MW01138460

I'm *Only* Here for the Beard

Book 4 of The Dixie Warden Rejects MC

By

Lani Lynn Vale

**ISBN-13:
978-1546812883**

**ISBN-10:
1546812881**

Dedication

This one is dedicated to my mom. Thank you for everything you do. Nobody said that you had to take my car in to get the oil changed, or pick my kids up from daycare, or fold my clothes because you knew I'd never get to it that day. But you did. You do everything that you can and more for me, and for that I'm the luckiest girl in the world.

Acknowledgements

My editors, Asli, Kellie, and Danielle—These books wouldn't be the same without y'all.

My beta readers—Leah, Barbara, Amanda and Jo. I love that you love my books as much as I do.

Cover model:

Photographer: Golden Czermak/ Furiousfotog

CONTENTS

PROLOGUE

Roses are red, violets are blue. Blah blah blah. I don't like you.
-Naomi's secret thoughts

Naomi

"Please talk to me."

I looked over at my brother, then shrugged.

My brother. The man who I once called one of my best friends had ruined my life.

He was in a bad place. I knew that. My mom and my current best friend, Aspen knew that. Hell, my dad even knew that and he wasn't even talking to me.

But did that excuse him for driving drunk? *No.*

"I'm not mad at you, Danny," I lied. "I'm just tired."

And I was. Tired. Very, very tired.

Though, I couldn't decide if that was due to the fact that I'd just clawed my way out from the haze of anesthesia or because I was just plain tired.

"Danny," my friend, Aspen, stated, "I think you need to give her some space. She's tired. She's confused, and honestly, she likely doesn't really want to talk to you right now."

What my best friend didn't say, however, was that he should feel guilty. I should be mad at him.

He'd hit me with his goddamned car!

And I wasn't even going to go into the fact that he'd done it in his police cruiser, of all things. I still hadn't figured out why the hell he'd been in the cruiser in the first place since it happened in the middle of the night.

Though, the same could be said about me. Why had I been out in the middle of the night, walking down the road where the house that I was renting was located?

Why? Because I was a fucking loser. My life sucked. Every man I met either cheated on me or found another woman to be with who they liked more than me. I was always the consolation prize. The rebound fling. The woman who men felt sorry for and had pity sex with.

Yeah, I was that girl.

So, fuck yeah, I was out in the middle of the night walking my street. Why? Because I couldn't fucking sleep. All of my insecurities had come out to play last night, and I'd stupidly gotten up, put on my running shoes and started walking.

The only problem with that? I'd gotten hit by my brother in his police cruiser when he was supposed to be at home.

I couldn't remember anything after actually seeing the car coming at me. Which was a good thing and a bad thing, I guess.

I couldn't remember the look on my brother's face when he realized he'd hit his sister.

I could, however, see it now, and it was heartbreaking.

He'd sank to rock bottom, though it was his fault.

Once upon a time, Aspen and Danny had been together. But my brother, being the idiot that he was, had cheated on her with his partner. The same partner who'd broken up with him a week ago by doing the same thing to him that he had done to Aspen.

So he'd started drinking to forget the fact that he thought his life was ruined.

Now, it really was.

He'd been suspended from the police department and was facing criminal charges. Not to mention that he would forever have to live with the knowledge that he drove drunk and ran over his sister with his police cruiser.

"Okay," Danny murmured. "If you need anything, call me."

With that my brother left, but I doubted he went much further than the waiting room. He'd been at the hospital since the accident had happened.

"Did you want to see it?"

I shook my head at Aspen. "No, I most certainly do not want to see it."

The 'it' she was referring to was my colostomy bag.

When my brother had hit me, I'd suffered damage to my intestines, liver and one kidney.

The liver and kidney were expected to make full recoveries.

My intestines, however, were going to require more time to heal, hence the latest addition to my wardrobe: a colostomy bag.

I could feel it.

It felt utterly foreign, like something was duct taped to my belly and just sitting there, waiting for me to take it off.

But I couldn't. At least not for another four to six months, according to my doctor, while my intestines had a chance to heal from the trauma I'd endured.

I'd have to be changing poop bags for six whole months.

Just when I thought my life couldn't get any worse, this was thrown at me.

Thank you, Danny, the life ruiner.

"It's not that bad," Aspen started to say.

I held up my hand. "Save it."

"The doctor said you could go back to work in six weeks," Aspen continued as if I hadn't just told her to shut up. "And Kilgore Fire would love to have you back. They're missing you already."

I was sure they were, but that was only because I took all the shifts that opened up or filled in whenever they needed someone. Now, they had to find someone else willing to pick up the shit shifts or come in at a moment's notice.

Though, if I were honest, they were about to have to start doing that anyway, because I'd made a decision last week, and I was going to stick with it.

"Aspen," I started, "I have to tell you something."

The drugs were wearing off, and my stomach was starting to hurt. That didn't stop me from telling my best friend something I should've told her a few weeks ago when I'd gotten confirmation from the new ambulance service where I had applied.

"What?" Aspen yawned, leaning forward.

I watched her as her jaw cracked with how wide she'd opened her mouth. Had I been in a livelier mood, I would've poked my finger into her mouth like I always did when she yawned, but I was tired and could barely find the strength to lift my head, let alone my hand.

I was depressed.

I'd been depressed for a while now, which had sparked the idea to move.

I'd looked all over the country for a job, and I had finally found one that would hopefully work well for me.

In Alabama. Six hours away.

"I'm moving."

She looked at me like I was crazy. "You're not moving. You're in bed."

I rolled my eyes heavenward and tried to shift in the bed.

Pain exploded in my body as aches and pains from my involuntary tumble against the hood of Danny's cruiser made themselves known.

"Sit still," Aspen said worriedly, helping me put the pillow that'd slipped out from under my head back where it needed to be. "You're okay."

I drew air in through my mouth, trying to control the pain with deep breathing since the pain meds I was on didn't seem to be helping.

"I said," I breathed carefully, "that I'm moving…not right now, but in a few weeks. To Alabama. Mooresville, Alabama."

Silence.

If there were crickets, they'd be chirping right now in the silence that followed my announcement.

"You're what?" Aspen worded carefully.

"I'm moving," I repeated, finally looking over at her.

She was flabbergasted.

I'd stunned her with my news, and clearly not in a good way.

"You can't move!" she cried loudly.

I hissed a breath at her. "Shhh!"

She ignored me, got up and began pacing the length of the small room.

"Oh, my God. I can't believe you're doing this to me. How could you?"

My brows rose.

"It's not like I just told you I was going to kill myself," I informed her. "I'm only moving."

"How many hours away is that?" she asked.

I bit my lip. "About six and a half."

She stared at me blankly.

She would've had more to say to that, too, but I was saved by a knock on the door.

Relief poured through me that I had this small reprieve from explaining my motives, until I saw PD and Aspen's husband, Drew, walking through the door and my heart sank.

Drew was awesome. I loved Drew. He was good for my friend. He loved and cherished her and he took care of my best friend like she deserved to be taken care of.

It wasn't Drew who made my heart hurt, though. It was PD.

PD was my crush...or had been before he'd gotten back together with his wife, July.

Now I was just that pitiful woman who everyone felt sorry for at work because they knew that I had—still have—a crush on a man who is taken. Thoroughly and happily taken at that.

Why PD was even here right now was beyond me. I knew it couldn't be because he was worried about me...though, I guess that maybe he could be but I doubted that was the case.

I had my answer a few moments later when he looked at me with pity filled eyes.

"How ya' feeling?" PD asked.

I shrugged, and I could've screamed at myself had I had the energy.

God, that hurt.

"Fine," I choked out. "What's up?"

Why are you here? Don't you have a wife to be at home with?

"I wanted to drop by and make sure you were okay…and also pick up the spare key to the quint."

I winced.

"In my purse over there," I pointed out, indicating the chair that was in the corner of the room.

My mother had dropped all of my things off on her way to work a half an hour ago. She stayed long enough to order the doctor to keep me well medicated.

That was my mother, though, helpful and shit.

Not that she really cared if I was well medicated. More like she wanted me to be well medicated and in a good mood in the hopes that I might allow her to borrow my car while I was in the hospital this week since I couldn't use it.

And *that* was going to happen over my dead body.

PD turned and walked over to my purse. He picked it up and started to move toward me, but I waved him off. "It's in the pocket on the inside."

Then I closed my eyes.

"You're moving?"

I cracked open one eyelid and stared at the big man across the room.

"Yep," I confirmed.

"When?" he asked.

I let my eye fall closed. "As soon as fucking possible. Somewhere where I can freakin' breathe."

Then I passed out, missing the hurt that crossed over both PD's and my best friend's faces.

PROLOGUE 2

Women are basically natural disasters with tits.
-Sean's secret thoughts

Sean

"This isn't about you, it's about me."

Wasn't that the quintessential line that every person used just before they broke up with their significant other?

Was I damaged? Was I that man who was destined to never have a woman who stayed with him?

I was a man who drank too much, laughed too loud and loved hard. That was why when I found a woman that I wanted to hang my hat up with, I put my all into it.

And always failed.

It didn't matter if it was good and we hadn't had a single hiccup. If there was a way to ruin the relationship before it even really came to fruition, I could do it. I have never, not once, been able to have a healthy relationship.

I thought I had that with Ellen, but here she was, proving me wrong.

Not even five seconds ago she'd told me that she couldn't do this anymore. That I was a good guy and that I deserved someone who could love me for me.

At least she didn't know that this was my fourth such breakup, or she would've felt even worse.

And I could tell she felt bad about it.

"Is there someone else?" I found myself asking.

I shouldn't have asked that. But there was always someone else.

Someone was always better than me, and to be honest, I was fucking tired of being second best.

Just fucking once I wished I could find a woman who wanted me for me.

I held up my hand. "Don't answer that."

I knew there was. I didn't miss the covert glances that she and Jessie James, the newest member of The Dixie Wardens MC Alabama Chapter, tossed each other.

I didn't miss the way Ellen always asked about him, or he about her.

Fuck me, but I was so fucking over it.

It was good that she'd called it off. I wouldn't have done it. I would've just stayed in a miserable relationship for eternity if it meant having someone there who cared about me.

But caring about someone and being in love were two different things, and I needed to realize that or I'd lose myself.

Ellen snapped her mouth shut and nodded once.

And without another word, I walked out and didn't look back.

CHAPTER 1

Women do not want to hear an apology while your penis is still inside their sister. Take it out first.
-Pro Tip

Sean

I rode my bike up to the spot where I usually parked and cursed when I went to turn in because a car was parked there.

"What the fuck?" I grunted behind my helmet. "That's my spot."

Okay, it wasn't actually my spot, but I'd been parking there for the last four years, each and every time I came to work.

Placing both feet onto the ground, I walked the bike backward and put it into the spot across from my usual and shut it off.

My helmet was the next thing to go, and I sighed when the open wind hit my overheated face.

Fuck, it was hot for the last day of October!

Shouldn't it be cooler already?

"Workin' out today?" a colleague, Randa McCullen, asked as she started walking toward her car.

I looked over at Randa, the basic EMT, and nodded. "Already done."

She rolled her eyes and shook her head. "Figures."

Then she walked straight to her car. Once there, she got in, waved goodbye, and closed the door before backing out of the spot and rocketing out of the parking lot.

I guess that meant she was ready to go.

Certainly would've wished I was leaving instead of just arriving.

Though, that was my usual lately.

I was working too much. The station I was working in for Allegiance Health was short staffed, and they mandated that every able-bodied paramedic had to work overtime whether they wanted to or not.

The only good thing I could say about my shift was that they ran a double medic truck instead of a single medic and a basic EMT. Otherwise I'd be so fuckin' tired from doing everything on every call while I was on shift that it'd be nearly impossible to hold down a job here.

Though, the pay was better than most.

Although, that wasn't saying much seeing as I made about four bucks over minimum wage, and I was working my ass off for it.

Every time I arrived for my shift, I couldn't come up with a single reason why I was doing this fucking job.

But get me in the back of an ambulance, and I forgot that my job sucked for the hour that it took to take the call.

I walked into the door of the station, and my eyes immediately honed in on the heart-shaped ass in a pair of the company's tactical pants swaying back and forth in front of the counter that divided the kitchen and the living area.

I closed the door a little harder than necessary in my surprise at seeing that ass, and winced when she turned around, her hand flying to her chest as if I'd startled her.

Which, I supposed that I did.

"Hi," I murmured.

The woman was short. Really short. Though, that didn't mean much when I was six foot four inches.

She had a head of blonde curly hair that was stuffed into a bun at the top of her head. A teal band was tied around her head to keep her curls out of her eyes—eyes that were so freakin' captivating that I wanted to blurt out an 'are they real?' to her.

She looked very standoffish, though, so I decided to wait to bombard her with questions until she at least knew me.

I was an intimidating guy. At least that's what I've been told.

People who knew me, though, knew that I wasn't going to hurt them.

Unless they deserved otherwise.

The woman smiled at me, but didn't offer me a 'hello' in return.

I walked inside and headed to my room, stopping when I saw that my room had already been taken.

"You're gonna have to move your shit," I told the woman over my shoulder. "This is my room."

The swift inhalation of breath had me turning.

"I'm sorry," she apologized. "That woman that just left, Randa, told me that this room was free."

She had a husky voice. One that instantly had me wanting to hear her whispering dirty words to me in the darkness of my bedroom.

"Randa's a bitch," I growled. "She likes to fuck with people because she thinks she's funny, but she's not."

The woman brushed past me, and I groaned at the smell of apples and cinnamon that wafted off of her.

Either she'd just eaten something or she had a lotion that smelled like heaven. Either way, I wanted to smell more.

She'd probably feel great...

Jesus fuck, that was the last thing I needed.

After Ellen had ripped my heart out three months ago, I couldn't do the dating thing again. At least not yet. Not after all the shit she'd put me through.

My phone buzzed in my pocket and I winced.

It was either Memphis or Ellen, and I didn't want to speak to either one of them at this point.

They were both concerned with my well-being. Whether I was coping well with the break up.

They were both good friends now, but I couldn't complain to Memphis, my childhood best friend, without wondering whether Memphis would be on my side or not.

So I chose not to talk to either one of them.

"I knew someone was in here. I should've gone with my gut," the woman muttered under her breath. "Thank you for not freakin' out."

My brows rose. "I wouldn't freak out over something so trivial," I informed her. "Now steal my cookies that I brought for dinner and I can't make that same promise."

She graced me with a smile and I forgot how to breathe.

She really was beautiful, even in the ugly white shirt that Allegiance made us wear.

It looked like it swallowed her whole, and I wondered if the one she was wearing was donated like my first one had been. At least her pants looked new.

The company was slowly transitioning to blue tops and blue bottoms with a white reflective stripe down the sides.

And fuck, but what looked butt ass ugly on most women, she filled out like a goddamned wet dream.

Even her little tactical boots were cute. I didn't realize that women's feet came in such a small size. Was she even in adult footwear?

"Can you even lift a person?" I found myself asking.

She froze, turned to face me and nodded her head. Her hands were wrapped around all of her things that she was hastily shoving back into her bag, and I nearly laughed at how pissy she looked.

"I'm sorry. It's just that you're tiny. I was curious." I held my hands up, dropped my backpack to the ground and walked back to the living room where I parked my ass in my favorite chair right in front of the TV.

It took her ten more minutes of moving her things before she joined me, and by the time she sat on the couch I was curious if she had something against men. She kept staring at me like I was going to jump up and bite her.

I flipped to my favorite station and had just put my hands up behind my head when the tones dropped.

Every fucking time.

Get comfortable? Tones drop.

Taking a shit? Tones drop.

Getting gas? Tones drop.

Eating out? Tones drop.

Sighing, I slowly let the foot of the recliner down and walked behind the woman who was about ten steps in front of me.

She was in the passenger seat of the medic when I got there and I smiled.

I did *not* ride in the passenger seat if I wasn't in the back. I hated it. Not having control of the wheel literally drove me fucking nuts.

That'd also been why I'd requested this particular shift with another medic so I wasn't stepping on any toes with the basics who were usually the ones to drive.

"Do you want to take lead?" I asked.

She looked at me and nodded, pressing the button that let our dispatch know that we were in the medic and on our way.

Okay then.

Did she speak at all? I wasn't sure.

Thirty minutes later, I secretly thanked the good lord above that she'd volunteered to take the call.

I turned the sirens on and accelerated slowly, being careful not to go too fast in case my partner, Naomi, (I had to get her name from her name badge because she still hadn't told me) was standing up in the back.

Which was likely since she was about to catch the baby that was about to fly straight out of the patient's vagina.

Maneuvering the streets of Mooresville, I made my way hurriedly to the hospital while still obeying most of the traffic laws.

I was thanking my lucky stars, too. In the nine and a half years I'd been a paramedic, I had not had to deliver one single baby, and I would hopefully keep it that way.

"Shit!"

Uh-oh. That didn't sound good.

"Oh, my God. Did I just poop?"

I winced.

"Don't worry, baby," the father that was riding in the passenger seat responded to his laboring wife. "The doctor said that was normal." He turned to me and whispered, "That's normal, right?"

I barely contained the urge to laugh.

"Yeah," I confirmed. "From what I hear, it is normal."

The soon to be daddy nodded, comforted by my words, and returned his gaze back behind him.

Did I relay the amount of relief pouring through me at not having to deliver this child?

I could do anything.

Blood, gore, exposed bone. Decapitated heads. Gunshot wounds. Vomit. Piss. Shit. But childbirth? Hell fucking *no*. That squigged me out.

As we passed the last street before the turnoff to the hospital, I heard the woman on the cot give an almighty screech, and then a few moments later came Naomi's 'you have a baby girl' as I was pulling into the bay.

I grinned at the father, who looked as white as a sheet.

"Ready, Dad?" I asked him.

He nodded, opened the door, and promptly fell on his face.

CHAPTER 2

*The closest I've come to double penetration is eating both Little
Debbies at the same time.
-Text from Naomi to Aspen*

Naomi

Oh, my God. Oh, my God, oh my God, oh my God!

I was shaking. Literally shaking.

This had been my very first shift without a training medic either
hovering at my side or available to ask questions—though, I was
sure if I'd run into trouble the sexy man who was my partner
would've helped.

Jesus Christ, but a man shouldn't be as sexy as him. It ought to be
illegal, because I couldn't stop myself from staring at him.

Surely, I wouldn't be able to function like this much longer.

Oh, God. *This place was supposed to get me away from hot men,
not put me into close quarters with them!*

I washed my hands thoroughly in the sink, splashed water on my
face, and then pulled down eight paper towels before roughly
scrubbing my face dry.

Holy shit, I'd just delivered a baby!

Once I was as composed as I was going to get at this point, I lifted my shirt up and checked out my new reality…at least for the next few months until I could have the surgery that would reverse it.

Testing to make sure the bag was secure, I sighed and tucked it back under the shirt that I wore to help hold it in place.

Then I tucked my clean shirt in, shoved my dirty one into a Wal-Mart sack and then deep into the depths of my backpack.

Once I had the backpack settled on my shoulders, I opened the door and frowned at seeing my partner there, standing with his back to me, staring at someone like his heart was being ripped in half.

Frowning, I walked up to his side and asked, "What's wrong?"

He jerked away from me like I'd scalded him with hot water, then cursed. "Sorry. Nothing is wrong. Why would you say that?"

The big man was lying to me.

I knew it with absolute certainty.

I studied his profile as he returned his gaze across the room. To a woman.

The woman was in front of the hospital reception desk standing next to a man that looked to be one of the doctors that worked there. She had long brown hair that was French braided down her back, and she was wearing a pencil skirt and a white flowy blouse that was tucked into the top. She had a wide black belt that covered her waistband, and I hated her instantly.

She was the type of woman who would look good wearing anything.

She probably wore her hair down to the gym, too.

"Who is she?" I asked as if he hadn't just lied to me.

Sean sighed.

"An old girlfriend."

The emotion that was in those words made my heart hurt for him.

But not too much.

The man was drop dead sexy, built like a linebacker with a fucking smile that was so beautiful it hurt my heart to look at it. And that beard. God, a man with a beard was my weakness. It always had been.

"Your ex is in love with another man," I felt it prudent to point out.

He shot me a glare and started walking in the opposite direction of the woman and the man she was trying everything in her power to catch the attention of. Although, the man was trying very hard to ignore her. He'd, of course, seen us standing here. If I had to have my guess, that man was likely a cop and missed nothing.

"Do you know that man?" I asked Sean's back as he passed through the exterior sliding door.

"Yes," he grunted.

I hurried after him as his strides became faster.

I made it to the passenger door of the medic as he put it in reverse.

For a second there, I was worried he was going to back up and leave before I'd even gotten in, but he surprised me by staying put until I had my ass firmly planted in the seat.

What he didn't do was wait for me to put my seatbelt on. He was nearly to the intersection before I'd completely situated myself.

So, me being me, I blurted out my life story.

"I've fallen in love with four men over the course of my life," I whispered. "When I was eighteen, I met a man who was four years older than me. We hit it off, got engaged, and then he cheated on me with my sorority sister," I started. "When I was twenty-two, I met another man who I fell in love with. We were great until we weren't. He beat the shit out of me. When I was twenty-five, I met another man I adored. We hit it off, then three weeks into our relationship I found out that he was married with four kids." I steadied my breath. "It took me nearly four years to try again. And when I did, I watched as that man, who has become a very good friend that I never had a chance with, married another woman. So, yeah, you likely have some heartache on the horizon, but it's not going to hurt forever."

Or so I kept telling myself.

It'd been nearly a year since PD had gotten married to July, and it still burned to see them together. Still made my heart ache so much that it was hard to be around him.

"My wife left me."

I blinked, turned, and stared.

"What?"

"Thought she was pregnant, turned out she wasn't but we had already gotten married. It was stupid. Neither one of us loved the other. We cared for each other, yes, but it wasn't love. Not even close. She was a confrontational shithead, and it took me weeks to realize that we weren't going to work out. But I'd planned to try. Then I was deployed and was gone for six months. While I was gone, she really did get pregnant by one of my best friends. Got home to find them making house together, her belly swelling with their child. I'd apparently missed the letter telling me that she wanted a divorce. Though, I'm still wondering if she ever sent it in the first place."

I winced.

"When was that?" I asked.

His smile was not pleasant. "Let's see...that was my first deployment. I was twenty and she was nineteen."

I bit my lip and reached for the bar above the door to hold on. "What else?"

I could sense there was more.

"At the age of twenty-five, my third deployment, I left a girlfriend behind. Came back home to her shacked up in my house. With another woman."

I winced.

"My fourth deployment, I met another soldier. Her name was Masha. She and I hit it off great. We were dating by the time we were done with that deployment. But as we made plans to meet back up, I hadn't counted on the fact that she had a husband she planned on leaving for me. I broke up with her and then promised myself I wouldn't date another woman."

I laughed softly. "How'd that work out?"

"Not well," he muttered darkly. "I met Ellen a year and a half ago. I fell head over heels in love with her the moment I saw her."

"But..."

He pulled onto the road that led back to the station.

"But she didn't love me back," he answered simply.

I picked up one of the curls that'd loosened from my bun, and twirled it around my finger as I tried to figure out what to say to that.

"I'm not going to tell you I'm sorry," I answered. "I bet you hear enough of that."

He sighed.

"Yes," he agreed. "I hear it from Ellen. I hear it from my best friend, who became really good friends with Ellen over the time that she and I were together."

I felt instantly sorry for him.

"My best friend married a man who is very good friends with the man that I fell in love with." I one upped him. "I can't even talk to her now for fear that it will get back to him. And I not only had to work with him, but I also watched him get married and then have a baby. Not only did I work with him, but we had a lot of the same friends. I saw him and his wife and baby everywhere. Every single party or event."

"The woman, Ellen, she's the sister of one of my brothers."

My brows furrowed. "So, she's a…stepsister?"

Was that right?

He snorted. "No. Tommy Tom, Ellen's brother, and the man you saw standing next to her, isn't my actual brother. He's a member of the Dixie Wardens MC with me."

"Is that a motorcycle club?"

He nodded.

"We have a few of those around where I lived," I muttered darkly.

Not to mention that PD had ridden a bike and had nearly joined a motorcycle club of his own. The only thing that'd stopped him from doing it was that he didn't want to leave Kilgore to join.

"Most do," he said. "Motorcycle clubs are becoming a lot more popular ever since that show came out on TV. Most are legit. Some are just a bunch of dumbasses on motorcycles with bad attitudes who don't know the law of the land."

"And what is the law of the land?" I asked, sitting silently as he pulled into the bay of the station and shut the medic off.

He grinned. A full blown, teeth showing smile that would've knocked my socks off if I didn't have boots holding them on.

"That there is always someone bigger and badder than you are."

Then he got out and walked inside, leaving me in the seat of the medic trying not to lose my composure.

The man, with his killer grin and dark soul, had the potential to bring me to my knees…and that wasn't a good thing.

I couldn't do another heartbreak.

Not now. Not ten years from now. Not ever.

And I needed to remember that.

Lani Lynn Vale

CHAPTER 3

Someone asked me if I believed in soulmates, and I told them I couldn't even find my keys. What makes them think I could find my soulmate?
-Sean's secret thoughts

Sean

It'd been three whole weeks since I'd been partnered with Naomi, and three whole weeks had gone by where I went to bed at night thinking about her rather than Ellen.

There were good things about this and bad.

The good: I didn't wake up with my heart hurting anymore. I didn't go to bed wondering whether Ellen was sleeping with her arms around some other man. I didn't see Ellen and think that I was wronged. I could go into my clubhouse and look at Jessie James and not want to punch him in the face.

The bad: I was replacing Ellen with Naomi. I had a permanent hard on for a woman who made it clear she wanted nothing more than friendship. I was going into work with more eagerness to see her than the actual job I was about to perform. Oh, and let's not forget the best one yet. I was falling hard.

Love didn't agree with me. I always, and I do mean always, got burned.

If it was possible for a six foot four-and-a-half-inch ex-marine to suffer, I suffered.

"Do you need anything from inside?" Naomi asked as she hopped out of the medic and turned to look at me.

I looked down at her, clenched my teeth, and then nodded my head. "My usual."

She snickered, backed up, and closed the door.

I watched her walk away.

My eyes were on her ass.

The way it swayed with each step she took.

"Hey," I said to myself. "This is not a good idea. One of these days she's going to do the same damn thing as the rest of them do."

Which was leave me or break my heart.

And if I was being honest with myself, I was getting damn tired of it.

The phone in my pocket rang, and I answered it while watching Naomi walk into the bathroom and shut the door.

She did that a lot. Went to the bathroom. She was supremely self-conscious about it, too. She didn't like going at the station. Only did it where it was public and nobody would be able to single her out.

Though, I suppose that was a fairly normal thing.

Women were self-conscious. My sister was very ill at ease about what she let the men in her life know. Such as the act of using the restroom. She freaked out when we mentioned it in front of her, and God forbid you ever mention the fact that anything she did in there, stunk.

Though, as I liked to point out to her, everyone had to shit. Everyone.

But whatever. If Naomi wanted to act like she didn't poop, then whatever. She could be hiding worse things, like cancer or the fact that she was a drug dealer.

I settled into a chair and prepared to wait.

***

Naomi

"Hey!" I called through the bathroom door. "Are you going to be much longer?"

Silence.

"Sean!" I knocked again. "You've literally been in there for thirty minutes. I have to pee."

Nothing.

I rolled my eyes up to the roof and stared at it for a few long seconds before I walked away.

The man had a bathroom problem.

A serious one that kept him in there for over forty-five minutes a damn day, and most of the time it happened to be right when I had to pee like a motherfucker.

And with there being only one bathroom in the station, I was shit out of luck until he was done with his toilet time.

"Son of a biscuit eater," I grumbled as I walked to the living room and stared out the window with worried eyes.

I had to change my bag. I normally would do it while we were out in case someone happened to see it in the trash, but I didn't have much of a choice at this point. It was either change it or walk around with my shit slapping against my stomach.

Something I still wasn't used to even after months of having to deal with the shit. Literally.

And oh, my God. The stoma squeaks were the worst!

I'd managed to keep them secret, or quiet, by placing my crossed arms lightly over the stoma (the hole that led to my colon from the outside) but they were getting more frequent and louder by the day.

I'd even gone as far as to call my doctor back home and ask him what I should do about them, and the devil had laughed. *Laughed!*

With nothing else to do, I walked into my bedroom, tucked my shirt and undershirt up underneath my armpits, and gathered my supplies.

Once I was situated with all my supplies on my bed, I opened the plastic bag I planned to stuff my shit bag into, and got to work.

After trying to decide whether or not to use reusable bags, I decided on the smaller disposable bags since I didn't have time to clean the bags out, and I felt confident in my decision, even though they were on the costly side.

Also, I'd gotten more efficient at changing it over the past few months, and I even developed a little system to get the job done but I still managed to get shit dripping down my stomach despite my trying not to.

It took me ten minutes to change my bag, and when I was done, I looked at the Ziploc, wondering what in the hell I was supposed to do with it now.

The point of the Ziploc bag was to contain the smell, but that didn't mean that some didn't leak through despite my efforts.

That meant the kitchen trash was out.

The bathroom was out, too, since I hadn't heard the bathroom door open since I'd been in here.

So, with confidence that Sean would be in the shitter for another five minutes, at least, (yes I'd timed him) I opened my door, peeked out, and made a mad dash for the front door.

There was a dumpster there that would be a perfect spot to throw my trash into.

And it would've been great, too, had I not opened the door and ran smack dab into Sean's muscular chest.

It felt like hitting a brick wall.

"Fuck!" I whined, trying to disentangle myself from Sean—who'd caught me before I'd gone sprawling out on the pavement.

My hands were up by his head, the bag of poo thrown over his shoulder like a fucking shoulder bag.

And I was about to cry.

I was touching the man with my poop!

Of course, it was in a bag, but still! I was touching him with it.

Embarrassment surged through me and it took everything I had not to wrench out of his arms.

I didn't.

If I had, he would've seen what was in my hands, and that would've been awkward.

Instead, I made the hard decision to stay in his arms, and hope he didn't look over his shoulder.

"Where did you come from?" I bit my lip.

His eyes went down to my mouth, then up to my eyes, and then back again.

"I was looking for you," he said. "Was wondering if you wanted to go eat."

I released my lip and his eyes returned to mine.

"Yeah," I said breathlessly. "What's that?"

I pointed to the brick of the station with one hand.

When he turned, I threw my bag as far as I could get it, watching it land at the back of the medic.

He frowned at me once he returned my stare.

"What was what?"

He looked over his shoulder, scanning for what he'd heard land after I'd thrown it, and saw nothing.

Thank God.

"I swear I saw something," I lied. "Where do you want to go eat?"

Please don't say Taco Bell. Please don't say Taco Bell.

"Taco Bell," he said. "It's either that, or Rudy's. And we've had Rudy's three times this last week."

I frowned.

We had.

But when it was either Rudy's or Taco Bell, I chose Rudy's every time.

But I was beginning to think that Sean wasn't under the same mindset.

"Don't we have to stay within our district?" I asked hopefully.

Taco Bell was about a quarter of a mile out of our district, and we weren't technically allowed to go there.

I secretly hated the other two stations because they had all the food in their districts, leaving Stupid Taco Hell and Rudy Doody's in ours.

And since I was a firm believer in sleeping as long as possible in the morning, I rarely, if ever, had time to make my lunch in the morning before I was expected to leave at oh, dark thirty.

"No," he answered. "I called Bill to make sure it was okay. As long as we eat in the medic, we should be fine. And I'll go in afterward to get us a refill for the road."

Resigned now, I reluctantly pulled out of his arms, feeling the loss of warmth almost instantly.

Shivering at the remembered warmth, I turned on my heels and started walking in the direction of my room, vaguely realizing that the light was on in the bathroom, but the door cracked clearly showing me that Sean was no longer in there.

"You could've at least turned the light off," I called over my shoulder at him.

He grinned unrepentantly and walked to the bathroom, retrieving his phone off the counter and his wallet off the floor as I retrieved my own phone off my bed and returned my supplies to my duffel bag and zipped it up.

"What was all that?" he wondered.

I turned to find him standing in the entranceway to my room, watching me zip the final length of zipper.

"Uhhh," I hesitated. "Papers I was going over."

His eyes lit up.

"I know medical supplies when I see them," he drawled. "I've been a paramedic for ten years now, and I was an EMT in the Marines for a few years, too."

So he realized I was lying to him.

Nice.

What do I say now?

He must've realized that I didn't want to say anything, though, and let me out of it.

"If you don't want to tell me, don't tell me," he drawled.

I bit my lip.

"I don't want to tell you."

His grin got wider. "Fine. Let's go eat."

"Let's," I scrambled up and shoved my phone into my pocket as I headed for the door.

I snatched my purse along the way, which happened to have an emergency stash of supplies needed for stoma care, my Kindle, a few chargers, and my wallet.

"You should really fear for your back's health when you carry that thing around," Sean said as he held open the door.

My mouth tipped up into a grin.

"Yeah," I asked. "I'll have to file that under my 'I don't care' tab. It has a lot of shit in it I need."

"You haven't read that Kindle once," he said. "I can see it in there, too. It's that new Oasis one. Do you like it?"

"Yes, I do." I nodded my head. "It's lightweight, compact, and has a hella good battery life."

I walked to the back of the medic, and would've picked up the baggie, but Sean started the medic up and put it into reverse before I could.

I bit my lip, wondering if he'd see me take it to the trash or not, and decided to get it when we got home.

I did manage to kick it to the side so it didn't get ran over, however.

The moment I was in the passenger seat, I let my bag fall to the floor between my feet and tried not to stare at my trash that I'd left in the grass.

Sean didn't seem to notice, thank God, and backed out of the garage before shutting the door with practiced ease.

"Do you ever let others drive if you're not in the back?" I questioned him.

He shrugged. "No."

My mouth twitched. "Did you get wet on the way to work today?"

My eyes took in the gray skies that'd been pouring down water for the last six hours. It'd been raining when I'd woken up and now, four hours into my shift, it hadn't let up once.

The poor city, I'd heard, wasn't very accepting of the rain due to a flood that'd hit Mooresville about a year ago. A flood that the people of Mooresville, Alabama were still trying to clean up after.

Luckily, the rain wasn't meant to continue much past the late evening hours, and it was supposed to dwindle down into drizzling rain—a paramedic's worst nightmare—very shortly.

"Yeah," he grunted. "Though my leather covered me most of the way. I just had to change my pants—which I planned to do anyway."

"Gotcha. That must've been your first forty-five minutes in the bathroom this morning."

His eyes narrowed as he turned his head and glared at me.

"I can't help it. It takes as long as it takes."

My mouth twitched.

"Hmm," I murmured, reaching down for my phone as an idea hit me.

"Hey, today I saw something on Facebook about a Squatty Potty," I told him. "Have you heard about that?"

"No," he grunted. "Can't say that I have."

My grin spreading, I pulled out my phone and started typing.

"What are you doing?" he asked nervously.

I batted my eyes at him, causing his own to narrow on my face.

"There's something weird going on with your eyes," he said in a monotone voice. "Would you like me to check them out for you?"

I stuck my tongue out at him and went back to my typing.

"Google is my friend," I informed him, and grinned as I typed into the search bar 'things that help you be more comfortable on the toilet.'

And there, one of the top results, was the Shark Tank invention 'Squatty Potty.'

I clicked on the first link which took me to Amazon, and started reading the description to him.

"The Squatty Potty is a wonderful health aid for the entire family. The Squatty Potty helps you to eliminate faster and more completely by putting your body into a natural squatting position over your own toilet. Using the Squatty Potty during elimination will un-kink your rectum, taking your body from a continent mode to an elimination mode. This will speed up the elimination process therefore reducing the risk of toxic buildup of fecal matter left in your colon," I stopped and turned my eyes to look at him. "That's what you need."

He flipped me off and continued driving, heading straight for Taco Hell.

"This is a different concept at first, but once you get the hang of it, it'll become like second nature," I continued. "What used to take forty long minutes, with butt tingling numbness about halfway through, now is a quick in and out process that you won't have one single complaint about. Satisfaction guaranteed!"

He was shaking his head furiously, his cheeks becoming pink.

"You buy that for me and I will literally kill you. I'll bury your body in the woods outside my parents' place, too," he informed me.

I bit my lip and started laughing inwardly as I clicked the 'Add to cart' option on my phone.

In two quick pages of buttons and clicking, I had it shipped next day, and closed my phone.

"I don't know what you're talking about," I lied. "There's your turn."

He glared at me, slowing down as he did.

"I know how to drive," he informed me.

I shrugged.

"You missed the turn last night. And the night before that," I countered.

He sighed.

"Fuckin' A, you're worse than Ellen."

I narrowed my eyes on him. "Don't compare me to someone you hate."

His mouth quirked. "Why not, Nay Nay?"

I growled at him. "Do not call me Nay Nay, either."

He chuckled as he pulled into the lot of Taco Bell, then passed a spot only to back into it expertly.

"Do you back in everywhere you go, even on your motorcycle?" I asked as he put the medic into park.

He shrugged. "Depends on where I'm going. My house, no. I just pull into my carport. A restaurant, or the grocery store? Yes."

I pushed the door open and got out, heading straight for the door.

I also prayed that I would manage to not have any negative

reactions to my meal, but I knew that prayer was in vain. I just hoped we were at the station when it happened.

CHAPTER 4

You don't have to be crazy to be my friend. I'll train you.
-Friend checklist

Naomi

We were on the way back to the station when the first squeak happened.

I slammed my hands down, pressing my elbow into the stoma as the noises started to come randomly.

"What was that?" Sean asked, looking over at me with confusion.

They were definitely unusual sounds, especially if you hadn't heard them before.

At least they didn't sound like farts.

Which was, I guess, both a good and a bad thing.

"I didn't hear anything," I said. "What'd it sound like?"

I pressed down harder on my stoma, then bit my lip when a wet sound filled the quiet surrounding us.

"What was that?"

I closed my eyes as mortification rolled through me.

"Still unsure what it is you speak of," I lied.

Sean watched me carefully as he drove, periodically looking over at me, trying to figure out what in the hell was making all the noise.

And by the time we'd arrived at the station and my colon was finished releasing hell, I ran to the station front door, keyed in the code on the keypad, and ran to my room.

I was soaked to the bone with sweat, embarrassed, and nauseous.

I knew I shouldn't have eaten that shit!

"Dammit!" I snapped, looking down to see my soaking wet shirt hoping and praying that there'd been no leaks.

Lucky for me, there hadn't.

Unlucky for me, the lights went out when I was in the process of changing my colostomy bag.

After a quick search for my phone, I realized that I'd left it in the medic in my haste to get to my room.

Which left me with two options.

Call out to Sean, or try to go get the phone without him seeing me practically naked.

I chose option two.

An option that I quickly realized I shouldn't have chosen when I walked outside, grabbed my phone from the garage, and turned to find myself face-to-chest with Sean.

At least I had grabbed a washcloth and covered my bare stoma first before pressing down...just in case.

"Shit!" I gasped, pushing away from a very bare-chested Sean. "What are you doing?"

"I was out here looking for a flashlight. What are you doing out here?" he questioned as he moved to the side.

At least I thought he moved to the side. I couldn't really tell if he was completely out of the way, but I chose to think he was and pushed my way through the doorway, only to come up short when the lights came suddenly back on, and I was left standing there with my shirt off, and my stoma bared to the world.

"Uhhh," I slapped the washcloth with my glove covered hand back over my biggest embarrassment. "See ya."

He grabbed my arm before I could move away and twisted me, staring at my belly with an intense focus that I didn't like.

"What is that?" he demanded, pointing to where my hand covered my belly.

My stoma chose that second to let out one of its squeaks, and I closed my eyes as horror dawned upon me.

"Just tell me. It's not like I'm going to get mad at you for hiding something that you and I both know is nothing to be ashamed of," he said. "And I know it's something, because you've spent the last few weeks trying to avoid telling me you have an ailment. Trust me. I'm not stupid."

Sighing in defeat, I lifted my hand, and Sean's eyes left mine to travel down my body.

I did notice how he stalled at my boobs for a few short seconds before they continued their travel down my torso.

He stopped at my stoma, then bent down to look at it closer.

I pushed him away.

"I just ate Taco Hell, man," I told him. "I wouldn't get that close. Our luck it'll squirt you in the eye."

He went back to his full height, then grabbed me by the hand and led me back to my bedroom where all my supplies were on the bed waiting for me.

"Was this the thing you were trying to keep from me right before we left?" he questioned with a knowing smile.

I shrugged, not saying yes or no.

"I'll take that blush on your face as answer enough."

Then he went about helping me get my bag on, and I sat in stunned silence as he did.

"What…"

He laughed before I could finish.

"My mother had IBS. She had a colostomy as well. For fifteen years before she died of colon cancer. I've done this more times than I can count," he said, explaining before I could ask. "How did this happen?"

Danger, Will Robinson!

"Uhhh," I bit my lip as he fixed me up. "Why do you ask?"

Though I was uncomfortable at the thought of telling him how it happened, his knowing that I had it was actually a relief. Hiding it from people was freakin' exhausting.

He stood up, walked to the bathroom, and disposed of the gloves he was using before washing his hands.

I picked up everything else, shoving it into the nearly full kitchen trash before emptying it and setting the bag beside the bay exit so I could take out the next time we left.

Then I went to my bedroom, picked out a new t-shirt and undershirt, slipping them both on, before I walked back into the living room where Sean was sitting on the couch.

"I ask because I want to get to know you," he said. "It's what partners do."

He did have a very valid point.

"My brother hit me with his patrol car while he was drunk off his ass, and I sustained some internal injuries." I sank onto the couch beside him. "At first, they were worried I might lose a kidney, but it bounced back. A section of my bowels was too damaged to be saved, though, and they had to remove that portion of it. It needs some time to heal, and in the meantime, I'm stuck with this."

He blinked at me.

"Your brother hit you with his patrol car while he was drunk."

It wasn't so much a question as it was him repeating what I stated, so I stayed silent.

"How much longer do they expect that'll take to heal?" he gestured to my stomach.

"I have about another couple months left on my sentence. Less if things are healing well," I admitted. "I'm visiting the doctor next week, a new one who's based here instead of back home. He's going to determine whether or not I'm ready to have it reversed."

His eyes were curious and on mine, not on the TV that was blasting in the background.

"How long do they expect your recovery to take?"

I shrugged. "I don't know. A few weeks or so, I'd guess."

He frowned. "Damn."

My brows lifted.

"Why do you say that?"

I leaned forward, bringing one of the pillows off of the couch to my lap as I slowly started to wrap the tassels around my fingers, watching him think.

"I'll take some vacation," he finally said. "That way I don't have to

51

deal with anyone that I don't like."

My lip twitched.

"You'd take vacation just so you're not stuck with a partner that you don't like," I repeated. "That's dedication right there."

He shrugged.

"I'm old and tired of dealing with other people's misconceptions about me. I'm not hard to work with as long as I like you. Other partners have their own way of doing things. I'm guessing it's because you're so new to being a paramedic that you're more open to other medics' way of doing things."

"Meaning, I don't whine when you want to drive all the time and don't get offended when you open doors for me and always put your back to the wall so you can see the room."

He sighed.

"I…"

The tones dropped, and he got up off the couch, walking to the door where his shoes were waiting.

"Suspected woman in labor on the side of 225. Volunteer medics on the scene." The dispatcher's static-laced voice filled the air.

"Goodie!" I clapped my hands.

If I had to go out in the rain, at least I got to see something good instead of something gory.

Childbirths were definitely one of my favorite kinds of calls.

"It's yours," Sean said.

I rolled my eyes.

Sean had a problem with babies and birthing women. Something I'd figured out after the past few weeks of working with the man. If a woman even hinted at being pregnant, he was passing her off to me.

"I'll deal with the women hiding food under their breasts all day long, not to have to deal with a woman during childbirth," he'd informed me when I'd questioned him.

"Aye, aye, Captain," I saluted him.

He narrowed his eyes at me.

"Don't start."

I grinned and offered him a smile tossed over my shoulder. "Yeah, yeah, yeah."

***

Six hours later, our shift change showed, and Sean and I both walked out shoulder to shoulder, to the parking lot.

The sun was shining and our eyes were burning.

After delivering a baby on the side of the highway last night, Sean and I had non-stop calls the rest of the night.

I was seconds away from passing out, and I couldn't wait to get home to my bed.

Sean's next words stopped me cold, though.

"Want to go on a ride this weekend?"

Before I could say 'no, that's not a good idea,' my true feelings took priority, and I blurted out the first words that came to mind.

My brows furrowed. "Sure. Where?"

He grinned.

"To Bear's Smokehouse. Though, the ride's going to start in within the city limits and lead out of town."

My head tilted slightly toward the side.

"What else is this?"

He grinned.

"A biker bash," he informed me. "I'll pick you up at three."

With that, he was on his bike and starting it up, and I was left standing there watching him go, wondering if I was making a huge mistake.

CHAPTER 5

It's the most wonderful time for a beer.
-Not your average Christmas Card

Sean

I was nervous as fuck and couldn't figure out why.

She was my partner. She was my friend.

And I was falling for her.

Certainly not as fast as I'd fallen with my past girlfriends but falling for her nonetheless.

The only good thing I could see in all of this was that we were denying it with everything we had in us.

I don't know why I invited her. I used my days off to recoup from being with her for twenty-four or forty-eight hours at a time, but I'd wanted to see her. And since I was off for three in a row, and she was off for two of those and then partnered with another medic on Tuesday until I came back on Wednesday, I wanted to see her.

Hence, the reason I invited her to go on a ride with me.

It was also my way of showing everyone that I'd moved on from Ellen and the heartache she'd caused me.

Though, that heartache didn't feel like much of anything these days. Even when I saw Jessie James and her together.

They hadn't come out and said that they were a couple, it was a given. I'd known toward the end of our time together that they had a thing. It didn't take a rocket scientist to see the longing glances they had both been tossing at each other.

But now, with Naomi coming for a ride with me, maybe everyone would give me some fucking breathing room.

Everyone but Naomi, anyway. She could stay as close as she wanted.

"Where are you going?" my father asked.

I turned to him, wondering if he had his President of Dixie Wardens MC hat or his father hat on.

Either way I would've ignored him, but I didn't want them to leave without me.

"I'm going to pick someone up," I leveled with him. "Don't leave without me."

"You'll be on time, or I'll leave without you," he shot back.

I waved my favorite finger at him, causing him to growl.

"This better not be some dumb blonde that's only coming so you can prove to the club and Ellen that you've moved on."

That was my father talking.

I gritted my teeth and managed not to snap at him, then walked out the door with my fists clenched tight. Ignoring the way it hurt to have my own father like my ex more than he liked me.

I knew without him saying that Dad had hoped Ellen would be it for me. That Ellen would become mine, and then I'd start popping him out some grandbabies.

Unfortunately for him, and for me, that wasn't going to happen. At least not with Ellen.

I was so lost in my thoughts that I nearly missed the rest of the men that were already starting to fill up our narrow driveway.

"Yo," I mumbled, skirting around Aaron's bike.

His wife, Imogen, was standing at his side, her side leaning against Aaron where he straddled his bike.

"Hey, man," Jessie held out his hand. "Where ya' going?"

I didn't turn to face the man that was at my back. I had liked him at first, but now that he had the full devotion of my ex, it was hard to like him, let alone tolerate him.

The fact that he was sitting in my driveway right now was making my hands itch to punch the fucker in the face.

It didn't matter that he never did anything untoward while Ellen and I were together. I knew that she had it bad for the man, and it was enough to put me off of anything Jessie James for the remaining unforeseeable future.

"Gonna go pick up someone," I told him the same thing I'd told my father. "Be back in a few."

The only good thing I could say about this was that Ellen wouldn't be here.

Jessie was still trying his hardest to not rock the boat too hard, and he was also denying his feelings in deference to me, I assumed. Meaning that, Ellen wouldn't be on the back of his bike, and she also wouldn't be here to rub it in.

Thank God.

I already needed to explain to Naomi that I wasn't using her just to get back at my ex. I didn't need to have it rubbed in her face the entire ride.

Thirteen minutes later, I pulled to a stop in front of an older home that'd survived the flood last year.

It was located at the top of a hill and was a pier and beam construction to boot, meaning it had extra protection from the water since it was raised a foot off the ground.

It was also so old that I half wondered if it wouldn't have been a kindness to the house to be swept away in the flood water.

Alas, some people found the old shit beautiful.

Me? I just saw a fire hazard.

I was all for modern construction. The newer the better.

If it was new, there was less chance of shit going wrong.

Hence the reason I had a brand-new bike, and traded my bike in once every four years, if not a little earlier.

See, I'd done the old breaking-down-in-front-of-the-fucking-mall thing. I'd also broken down in front of the Brookshire's, the Taco Bell, the movie theater, and the most popular restaurant in town. All of which at least one of my friends had witnessed, giving them free reign to rib me after the fact.

So yes, I was over the 'will it pass inspection' thing and was all about reliability. Houses. Cars. Motorcycles. Didn't matter. If I could afford to buy new, that was what I'd get, or I'd wait until I could afford to buy new.

This house was a far cry from new.

I couldn't see Naomi living here comfortably, either.

It was old, run down, and I'd lay money down that it didn't even have reliable running water.

I could see a well house in the back that was likely the source of her water, and the power connected to the house looked like it would come down in a swift breeze.

"Morning," I rumbled as the devil herself exited the house and started toward me.

She didn't even bother locking up.

"You're not going to lock up the door?" I asked her when she made it off the last porch step.

She looked over her shoulder at the house, then shook her head.

"No," she informed me. "There's nothing in there to steal."

"Not a TV?" I asked.

She rolled her eyes. "I have my laptop under a blanket on the couch, which besides my Kindle, is my only source of entertainment when I'm at home."

"And let me guess," I eyed her big ass purse. "You have the rest of your life in your purse?"

She started to giggle as she walked down the path toward me, her eyes going to the ground to ensure she didn't trip on one of the fucked up boards lining the front walk leading to the fucked up house.

I chose to take a moment to take in her body.

She looked different without her uniform. More carefree somehow.

Though her shirt wasn't tight, it was shapely. It must've been a throwback from her high school days, because it said Kilgore Bullies Soccer 2006 over the breasts.

I couldn't see any other reason she'd be wearing it unless she'd played.

Her thighs, though…those were definitely soccer thighs. Even now, over a decade after that t-shirt was made, it was obvious she tried to keep in shape. Her legs were a tribute to her soccer days.

They were the type made for power. To get her where she needed to go as fast as she could get there.

And they'd look fucking amazing shoved up by her ears as I took her hard, my hands holding her knees hostage as I powered my hard cock into her willing body.

Luckily, those sexy legs were encased in a sturdy pair of jeans, otherwise I'd have to commit the ultimate sin and ask her to change.

As it was, I'd have to be giving up my leather jacket.

I couldn't risk that sweet, smooth skin of hers meeting the road and being torn off.

Not only would I feel terrible, it'd be a slap to mankind's face.

She was everything that I looked for in a woman, and it literally baffled my mind that she had man trouble. Some good man with the right intentions, unlike me, should have swooped in and swept her off of her feet already.

She should literally be birthing a man's babies, and making his life fuller than it already was.

Instead, she was walking toward me with a spring in her fucking step, unaware just what she was walking toward.

As I watched her take the last few steps, I made a decision.

I was done playing friends. I was done with my good intentions. I was also done fucking my life up.

No more would I allow people to use me. I wouldn't pick up any shift I could. I'd spend time with my girl – one who didn't know that she was mine yet. And I'd fucking level any guy who tried to take her from me.

I wasn't some pansy. I was an ex-Marine. I'd fought fucking wars.

And Naomi had the kind of face that drove men to start wars in the first place.

What I wasn't willing to do with Ellen, I was more than willing to do for Naomi.

I'd only have to prove it…and go slow.

Because I didn't want to scare her away. She'd been burned before and I wasn't willing to hurt her in any way.

"I like your shoes," I told her.

She stopped at the side of my bike and checked out her boots.

"I called my friend back home and asked her what she wore when she was on the back of her man's bike. She told me, and I had Amazon overnight these to me," she informed me. "I also got another present that's yours as soon as I can find out where you live."

I narrowed my eyes.

"You better not have…" I warned low in my throat.

She batted her beautiful blue eyes at me and grinned innocently. "I don't know what you're talking about."

Sighing, I offered her my hand. "Might want to move the helmet so it doesn't get stuck up your ass when you sit down."

She snorted, reached for the helmet as well as kept hold of my hand, and then shifted behind me, getting comfortable, before letting go of my hand.

My fingers tingled from where they'd come into contact with her skin, and I cleared my throat to keep the groan at the feel of her thighs around my hips in as she scooted forward.

"I had to ask my friend about this, too," she said. "Her name is Winter, and her husband's name is Jack. Winter worked at the fire department with me. Her husband's also ex-military. Army, though, not Marines."

"Pity," I drawled. "You'd been doing so well until you said what branch he's from."

She pinched my side and laughed.

I squirmed.

I was ticklish as fuck on my sides and she fucking knew it.

I'd stupidly told that to her on one of our long nights posting—also known as hell in limbo. Posting meant that we were positioned between two stations, ours and a neighboring one, waiting for an emergency in either district at the gas station forty miles away from our station. Though she'd also told me that she was ticklish under her chin and boobs.

At the time, I wasn't willing to find out if it was true or not.

It was a completely different story now, though.

"That would've been funny had you not sounded so absolute about it being a shittier branch than you were from," she laughed.

I found myself grinning despite trying not to.

"I can't help it that all other branches are inferior to the Marines," I informed her.

She sighed and started fiddling with her helmet.

I watched her out of my rearview mirror as she fitted the helmet onto her head.

It was brand new, one I'd bought specifically for her, and it fit her perfectly.

Hot pink with a white stripe down the top, it also had faux white fur glued to the stripe which made it look like she had a white Mohawk. She looked absolutely adorable.

Adding in the pale blonde curls that peeked out from underneath, and I was hard as a rock.

But it also might've been because she kept grinding her hips into my backside.

"Ready, Freddy?" I asked her, letting my hand come to a rest on her knee.

She breathed out shakily.

"Yes, Sir," she teased.

Exhilaration tore through me.

"Those are the magic words," I told her, then started my motorcycle up.

The ride back to the house was an easy one, made easier by the way Naomi took to riding. It was clear she'd never been on a bike before, but she was a quick learner.

I took turns, and she held on tighter, letting her body sway with the bike.

She also didn't freeze up when someone pulled out in front of us, or braked too hard like most people would.

She was just there, enjoying herself, while wrapped around me.

And by the time I arrived back home, I was fairly positive that the next four hours were going to be an agonizing form of torture.

As I got off and offered Naomi my hand, I surreptitiously adjusted my very hard cock behind the fly of my jeans and tried to look anywhere but at the men I could tell had been watching the move.

"About fuckin' time," Tommy Tom grumbled as he got up off the bench that was in our front yard and started toward us. "I'm starving."

I looked at my watch. "It's ten in the morning. You should've already had breakfast by now."

He shrugged. "I actually had breakfast at about three this morning. Something that I'm sure you're well aware of since you saw me there."

I had. I'd picked up the back half of a shift yesterday due to a colleague calling in sick.

I'd brought a patient in at three that morning. And again at four, five, and six.

By the time shift change rolled around at six thirty, I was more than ready to head home and catch a few hours of shut eye before the ride was supposed to start.

I'd also overslept, and had texted Naomi once I'd woken up that I was on my way, and not to freak out because I hadn't forgotten about her.

She'd sent me a quick text in reply that she'd been sleeping, too, and that it wasn't a big deal. She was going to head into the shower, and she would see me when I arrived.

Which led to now, all the men surrounding us, watching and waiting for me to introduce the woman who'd ridden in on my bike.

Something that not many women had the privilege of doing in the past.

"Nay Nay…"

Naomi pinched me. "Don't you dare."

I grinned and winked at her, causing her to sigh and turn back to the full driveway.

"My name is Naomi," she introduced herself to the group as a whole. "Don't let him tell you otherwise."

Aaron's wife, Imogen, walked forward and extended her hand. "My name is Imogen. That man back there scowling at the world is my husband, Aaron. This is Tommy Tom and his wife, Tally. That's Truth. His wife, Verity, is heading to the smokehouse in her

64

car since she's newly pregnant, and these men somehow revert back into cavemen mentality when one of us winds up pregnant."

She widened her eyes at Naomi, who smiled in reaction.

"That's nice to know," she admitted.

It was also true. Pregnant ladies didn't ride, and every single one of the members of our club felt the same way about it.

I'd seen way too many bad things happen to the passenger on a bike to take the risk.

Which got me to thinking about what Naomi would look like pregnant. Would she be like Imogen, who'd just had her second child, and looked like she'd swallowed a basketball toward the end of her pregnancy? Or would she be like Verity who gained a shit ton of weight, but still managed to look like she was glowing throughout?

I hoped she was one of a kind. I couldn't wait to see her belly swelling with my child…whoa!

Where that thought had come from, I didn't know. But I stopped it before it could get too rooted in my brain. There wouldn't be any babies in my future, at least none that I could foresee right now.

I wanted to take it slow and really get to know each other. Then in a few weeks when—yeah, I said when—I finally get her into my bed, we'll already be committed to each other. I'd make sure that we were solid and in it forever before we brought any kids into the picture.

My father pushed through the crowd, a big grin on his face when he saw Naomi at my side.

"Naomi," I took her by the arm and turned her gently around to face my father. "This is Big Papa, the president of the Alabama chapter of the Dixie Wardens MC and my father."

Naomi took the man in for a few long moments before she offered her hand to him.

"It's nice to finally meet you." She shook his hand. "Sean has a lot to say about you."

Dad's mouth quirked up at the corner. "I notice that you aren't saying that he has good things to say about me."

Naomi's mouth thinned into a line as she bit her lip. "I don't know what you're talking about."

Dad laughed.

"It's nice to finally meet you as well. Sean really has had nothing but nice things to say about you."

Naomi looked at me with a flare of excitement in her eyes. "Well of course he has! I'm a perfect angel."

That's when the UPS driver pulled up in front of our house.

I turned, wondering what my father had ordered, when I saw a flash of curly, blond hair making a mad dash for the truck.

Then a thought occurred to me.

"That better not be what I think it is!" I bellowed at the woman who was taking the big box from the driver's hands and jiggling it excitedly.

"I don't know what you're talking about," Naomi laughed as she dropped the box to the grass just past the road, dug into her pocket to pull out what appeared to be an EMT's pocket knife, complete with tactical shears, and easily cut the box open.

"Don't you dare," I warned her.

Naomi batted her eyes at me innocently.

"I don't know what you're talking about," she repeated.

Then she pulled out the fucking stool thing that she'd told me about a few days before when she read the description aloud to me.

"I thought you said you needed my address," I replied neutrally, hoping like hell that she didn't show off the item to everyone currently watching her like she was an amusement show. Also hoping that she didn't let everyone know about my unusually long bathroom habits.

I was, of course, unhappy to see that she did pull out the item. Then launch into a long, drawn out discussion about my less than ideal shit times.

"So, this all started when I began working with Sean a few weeks ago. He takes forever to…*you know.*" She grinned at Imogen who'd walked up and taken the step like contraption from my woman's hands. "And so I Googled 'things to help you poop,' and came up with this beauty."

"What is that?" my dad asked as he walked over, too.

"It's called the 'Squatty Potty'. It was on Shark Tank, and it is supposed to help make it more comfortable and quicker when you…errrrmmm…poop."

I was now thoroughly convinced that I needed to spank her.

I wasn't talking about a purely pleasurable little spanking either, although I'm sure that with my hand on her ass, it would definitely turn into that.

I probably needed to do something to shut that mouth of hers up, too. Possibly involving my dick. Or maybe just her face shoved into the pillows while I fucked her hard from behind would work. That way I could keep a good hold on the back of her head to be sure that she couldn't move from where I'd placed her.

This, of course, was my inner caveman talking.

I didn't actually want to do any of that…oh, who am I kidding. All of those things sounded incredibly appealing.

Especially when she handed the Squatty Potty over to my father and ordered him to *'put it where Sean poops.'*

I rolled my eyes heavenward, and Truth, my club brother and a really good friend, came up to my side and slapped me on the back. "Women are awesome, aren't they?"

"Very," I drawled sarcastically. "Is there any reason that you can come up with for why I should refrain from spanking her ass? You teach baby cops to become big cops. Any laws that I should be concerned about?"

Truth snorted. "A few, but I'll cover you, and I know a few guys who'll play ignorant."

I grunted in reply and walked over to Naomi, offering her my hand. "I'll be talking to you about this later. In the meantime, we have a deadline to get to the smokehouse, otherwise they'll all turn around, and we'll miss the ride."

Naomi grinned widely at me. "Yes, Sir."

The way she said 'sir' had my cock straining against the seam of my pants again as I pushed down the urge to pull her into my arms and slam my mouth onto hers.

I didn't do either of those things. Instead, I bit my lip and curled my hand around her small bicep, thinking that God clearly was torturing me for some reason.

I'd obviously done something to displease him.

"Let's go," I ordered.

She pulled her arm out from my grip and then ran toward my house, heading where my father had just disappeared inside.

"I have to check this out," she said. "Just give me two more minutes."

I ran after her, caught up to her, overtook her, and then turned and planted myself in front of her. The moment she stopped, I bent forward, picked her up, and tossed her over my shoulder. I was careful not to put her weight on her ostomy side, and marched straight toward my bike, passing my brothers and their wives, who were all laughing their asses off.

"Shut it," I grumbled as I passed them.

Tommy Tom took his seat on his bike, followed shortly by me on mine.

The rest of them followed suit, and then, eventually, so did my father.

"That better not be in my bathroom," I grumbled at my father.

My dad didn't say a word as he mounted his own bike and started it up.

Finally in place, I set a laughing Naomi on her feet and glared at her. "Get on, Nay Nay."

She bared her teeth at me.

Reaching out, I enclosed her small wrist in one of my hands and pulled her forward.

She came forward on a gasp, and when she was only inches away I moved my face in to meet hers and said, "Spankings. Lots and lots of spankings."

She grinned, and I broke.

I couldn't help it.

I pulled her the last few inches to my mouth and slammed my mouth down on hers.

She tasted like fire.

Fucking fire.

Cinnamon and something else that made me want to stay buried in her mouth forever.

But I couldn't.

Mostly because engines were starting, and my club was yelling at me to 'get a room' and 'be off' at the same time.

I let her up and her cheeks were flushed.

Blonde curls were scattered all over the place, and I grinned unrepentantly at her.

"Get on, baby."

She got on, and not another word was said for the next half an hour as we rode to the smokehouse.

CHAPTER 6

Do you ever look at someone's kid and think 'this one is going to be an asshole when he grows up?' Yeah, me too.
-Naomi's inner contemplations

Naomi

I was in hog heaven, literally and figuratively.

Literally, because I was surrounded by no less than a thousand motorcycles. A full lot in front, and just as much in the back. All of them were loud, and I was having the time of my life.

Figuratively, because I was on the back of Sean's bike, and he'd given me the kiss of a lifetime before we'd left.

I wasn't sure yet whether it was because he was mad at me or because he wanted me to shut up.

Either way, I was going to cherish that kiss for the rest of my life.

I was also going to do something bad. Very, very bad.

Which was sleep with my partner.

And I was going to enjoy every fucking second of it.

Sean hadn't come out and told me that he wanted to fuck me. In fact, all he'd really done was touch me—and not even inappropriately.

All that'd been done were slight touches. A brush of his hand here, a squeeze of my leg there.

All in all, it was really quite innocent.

But what made me sure that he wanted me was the permanent hard on that'd been tenting the front of his pants.

He'd been extremely cool about it, but it was near impossible not to feel it—or see it.

At the beginning of the ride, I'd had my arms cinched tight around his waist. But as time went on, and my arms became tired of holding on that hard, I let them slip to pool in his lap. *A lap that was housing a very impressive erection.*

At first I'd left it there, not sure whether I should move my hands and make it known that I knew he had a problem.

But then, as time wore on, I realized that I didn't much care if he knew that I knew he had an erection. So I stayed with my hands wrapped loosely around his tight belly, resting lightly against his jeans.

Jeans that fit so snugly that each time I actually looked into his lap, I could see the long thick column of his cock reaching down into the legs of his jeans.

The bike slowed, and I looked up and smiled at the woman beside me.

She wasn't one of ours. In fact, the biker girl leather jacket that she was wearing declared her part of The Uncertain Saints MC.

I waved at her, and she winked at me, picking her hand up to play with some of her hair that had slipped free of her hot pink helmet.

I'd started counting the bikers when we'd first started, and slowly decided that maybe counting wasn't going to work since we had so many surrounding us.

Instead, I started counting the different vests that declared which motorcycle club the men and women belonged to.

So far, I was at twenty-four different organizations. Only one of which I actually knew lived in the area—That being the Dixie Wardens MC.

Sean's body tensed, and I looked up to find that a few of the bikers in front of us had started braking, readying themselves to turn into the smokehouse that was just a few hundred feet ahead.

My ass gave a relieved thrum as I thought about standing up, but my vagina, which happened to like exactly where it happened to be at that moment in time, wasn't feeling the same tingly emotion.

It was upset. And I was, too.

I didn't want to get off the bike, because doing that meant I could no longer press my body against Sean's without looking like a complete and utter weirdo.

Sean braked a little harder, and I tightened my hands around his waist, holding on and leaning with his body while he took the turn into the parking lot.

I watched the ground pass us by, enraptured by the idea of nothing surrounding me.

Sean's body wiggled, and I held on even tighter as he came to a stop not at the front of the lot like some of the first ones in, but at the back.

He backed in, just like he always did, and made me smile into his leather vest.

"Shut up," he rumbled the moment he'd kicked down the stand and shut the bike off.

I grinned huge as I reached for my helmet, pulling it off of my head and saying a quick thank you to whoever had designed it. My helmet was the cutest thing I'd ever seen, and I couldn't believe that Sean had picked it out for me, all by himself.

"Legs Jell-O?" someone asked from beside me.

I turned to find Imogen and Aaron pulling into a parking spot directly next to ours.

"Yes," I said to Imogen. "I'm pretty sure that they wouldn't support my weight if I tried to stand right now."

Imogen reached her arms up high over her head, and Aaron chose that moment to drop down and blow a raspberry on her exposed belly.

Imogen laughed and brought her elbows down to protect herself, but only succeeded in elbowing Aaron in the neck, causing him to whine.

"Oww!" he fake cried.

I rolled my eyes and went to step forward, only for my leg to go out from beneath me.

Lucky for me, Sean was there to catch me. And catch me he did.

Then he went even further and pulled me straight into his arms.

I stayed there for a few long seconds, basking in the feel of his arms around my shoulders, before turning slightly in his arms to look up at him.

"This isn't a good idea," I told him. "I'm the queen of bad ideas."

His grin was wicked.

"If you're the queen, I'm the king."

And that was that.

He turned me in his arms, looped one arm around my waist to help me, and then started strolling with me to the front door of the smokehouse.

And it really was a smokehouse.

"Wow!" I hesitated, looking around at the huge room that was in front of us.

It was nothing but display cases. The food in the display cases was in order. Alligator. Antelope. Chicken. Elk. Moose. Pork. Venison.

And that was only a fraction of what was there. There were literally hundreds of different types of meats.

"Can you eat here?" I questioned, my eyes taking in all the display cases.

"I think so," he said, sounding unsure. "But I'm only looking for a bathroom."

I looked at him. "You need to go to the bathroom?"

He looked at me.

"No. But I know when you are on shift for more than three hours, you change your bag. So I'm finding you a bathroom so that you can do that."

He really was a lot more comfortable with the fact that I had a colostomy than I was, that was for sure.

He didn't seem weirded out about it in the least, and I actually found that quite sexy.

I was also appreciative.

"I think it's back there," someone said from behind us.

I turned to find a large biker standing there. His eyes were on me, and he was staring at me like he'd seen a ghost.

"Thanks," I said, smiling at the big man. "I appreciate it."

With that, I squeezed Sean's hand, shouldered my bag more

comfortably across my shoulders, and headed in the direction the man had pointed.

Unlucky for me, there was only one bathroom for the women, and one for the men, so I had to wait for a few minutes while the woman ahead of me finished.

And in that time, the big biker who'd directed me to the bathroom showed up at my back.

"Did you enjoy the ride?"

I tried not to flinch at the smell of alcohol that wafted off of the man.

"Yes," I said, bidding the door to open faster. "I did, thank you."

Why was there only one women's bathroom? For real, this was ridiculous.

There was now a line at my back, and the majority of them were women.

This would be fun…not.

"You have the prettiest blonde hair," the man said at my back. "Do you mind if I touch it?"

I smiled at him. "I don't like my hair to be touched, thanks. My man gets pretty jealous."

"Your man doesn't have a property vest on you, so he must not be your man," the biker countered, reaching forward.

Before he could get his hand to my hair, though, the bathroom door opened, and the woman that'd been holding up the line spilled out.

She looked green around the gills, and I wondered if she'd been puking in here, and would need it soon.

Hopefully not.

Though I'd gotten fast at changing my bags, I wasn't a master at it.

It took time that I didn't always have, and in this instance, with all those ladies waiting outside, I knew I'd make a muck of it.

It all went smoothly and I finished as fast as I could. Though I still guessed it was longer than anyone would've imagined.

Thankfully, there was a commotion in the hallway, and when I came out, they were all focused on the big biker rather than me.

The unfortunate thing was that he was bowing his chest up to Sean, who was trying to get into the bathroom behind the biker that was barring his way.

"Get the fuck out of the way, man. I have to take a piss."

"No," Big Biker, BB for short, denied. "You don't deserve to use the restroom."

He didn't deserve to use the restroom? What the fuck?

"You can use the women's," I drawled, trying to break the heated discussion I could see on the road to deterioration. "I'm all done."

Sean's eyes didn't come off of BB, but BB's eyes turned to me.

"Darlin'," BB drawled. "I would love to come in there *with* you."

BB wasn't hard on the eyes. He was tall, six foot or so. Brown hair, brown eyes, a long angular nose. Bushy eyebrows and a beard that was actually quite pleasant.

What wasn't pleasant was the vibe I was getting off of the man.

He just rubbed me the wrong way, and I didn't want to go anywhere near him.

"No thank you," I said, slipping around the men. "Sean, come with me."

Sean didn't budge until I was past him. The moment I was, he started backing away.

As I turned and moved toward the end of the hall, I was

unsurprised to find the rest of the Dixie Wardens at our backs. During the ride, they'd always been close. And thank God they were now, too.

Because I was fairly sure it would only take a single word from BB and Sean would lose it.

My fear-filled eyes latched onto Big Papa, Sean's father, and I gestured with my eyes and head for him to get his ass in gear.

His mouth twitched and his eyes warmed.

He did follow directions, though.

With a few steps in our direction, he broke the spell with one growled word.

"Sean."

Sean twitched, backed up, and then turned to the side so he could see his father.

I flinched.

Not only could his father see his face, but I could, too. And it was terrible.

He was angry. Very angry.

And his hands were clenched so tightly into fists that they were bloodless.

Something terrible was going on behind those eyes, and I knew that it couldn't be just about fighting with that man. And if it had been, there'd been more said than just the words I'd heard after coming out of the bathroom.

"Sean?"

Sean's eyes, filled with anger, turned to me.

It took him all of three seconds before he closed his eyes, seemed to come to some sort of understanding, and took a step forward.

Only to come up short when BB decided to take his drunk ass a step too far and launch himself at Sean.

Sean didn't even hesitate.

One second he was walking away, and the next he was hammering a vicious punch into BB's face.

BB went down like a stone, right at Sean's feet. He was out like a freakin' light.

The men around us, as well as the women still standing in the bathroom line, stared in stunned silence for all of five seconds before cheers erupted.

"He's drunk," one said.

"He better be drunk. Even I wouldn't mess with a man that big," another added.

"That rocker on the man's back was enough to deter me from doing anything," one more butted in.

I stared at Sean as he angrily stomped away, pushing through his own brothers and not saying a word as he went.

"Uhh," I hesitated.

Imogen held out her hand, and I walked forward.

She tagged me around the wrist and pulled me to Tally, who was trying really hard not to smile.

Tally started giggling.

"I've never seen him that mad!"

"Tommy would be mad as hell, too, had he said words about you like that man said about Naomi," Imogen whispered.

"I thought he was going to do a lot worse than just hit him," Verity added in her two cents. "Did you hear that part about BB and Sean sharing her?"

I shivered.

"Let me guess," I said slowly. "The man said stuff about me and Sean freaked out."

Imogen nodded. "Sort of. He got all quiet first. Then when he tried to go into the bathroom, and you showed, the man's eyes went all creepy like and Sean told him to 'be careful'." She stopped. "You know the rest."

I didn't bother asking what was said by BB. It was likely vulgar and it was best that I kept myself ignorant.

"Do you remember four years ago when Sean got pissed over that man stealing his seat in the bar, and then one thing led to another and Sean punched the guy like he just did a few minutes ago?" Tommy Tom asked Truth at my back.

I turned my head and studied Tommy Tom.

"It was the most beautiful thing I'd ever seen," Truth nodded. "One single punch to the jaw, and the man was out exactly like that. It's good to see he didn't lose his touch when he left the Marines."

I looked at Tommy Tom in confusion.

He noticed and started to explain.

"Sean used to be one of those Body Bearers for the Marines. They called him Beast while he was doing that. He was freakin' jacked," Tommy Tom explained. "He's actually slimmed down a lot since he got out of the Corps."

The man was *bigger?*

Jesus. He was already hard as a rock everywhere. I couldn't even begin to imagine what he looked like bigger.

"What's so special about being a Body Bearer for the Marines?" Imogen asked.

A man piped in that was beside us.

His biker patch said 'Griffin.'

"Because those guys are fuckin' beasts," Griffin said from where he was leaning against the wall in the hallway. "All other branches of the military use eight pall bearers for a funeral service. The Marines only use six. They carry the casket at elbow height, and they lift it to eye level and hold it there before it's lowered into the ground. They're not allowed to breathe out of their mouths. They're in perfect presentation at all times. Normally, that means they're out in the heat and sunshine, full fucking dress uniform."

That did sound hard.

"They really are pretty fuckin' awesome. And well respected. They train in a goddamned basement for hours a day to make it look perfect when they were at a Marine's funeral."

That sounded depressing, and actually kind of dedicated.

Hell, I was lying. That showed a lot of dedication.

Dedication that I sure as hell didn't have.

I didn't work out.

I should, but I didn't.

Why? Because working out made my boobs bounce so hard that they hurt, my legs shook, and my head throbbed.

Why work out when it hurt that much?

"Oh, shit."

I turned my head in the direction of the 'oh shit' and found Tommy Tom staring at something straight ahead.

My eyes automatically went in that direction to find Sean, his arms crossed and his jaw clenched, staring down at a woman with a blank expression on his face.

The woman, however, didn't have a blank expression.

She was talking animatedly to him. Her arms were waving, and she was poking him in the chest every so often.

"Who's that?" Imogen asked, stopping at my side.

I moved until I was nearly touching the glass that was separating the inside from the outside, and watched.

"That's his ex-wife," Truth grumbled. "She's the one that left him while he was deployed."

That was enough to get me moving.

One second I was inside and the next I was outside, heading in the direction of Sean with an angry scowl on my face.

"I don't know what the big deal was. We were eighteen."

I stopped at Sean's back.

The woman apparently didn't see me because she continued spewing her mouth.

"That was over fifteen years ago. Working on twenty," the woman continued. "And, honestly, I was scared. I didn't know if you were going to make it home and that scared the crap out of me."

Sean didn't say anything still.

So I chose that moment to wrap my arms around him from behind, locking my hands together right under his pecs.

The woman stopped mid-sentence as she saw my arms wind around Sean, and I smiled into his back.

Sean's massive hand—the same one that I'd seen put an IV into a six-week-old baby only four days before—wrapped around my wrist and held on tight.

I nuzzled my cheek against his back wondering if it would be okay to do this while naked, and waited for the woman to continue her rant.

She didn't.

Instead, the silence surrounded us, and I sighed.

Moving from where I was, I walked around the left side of Sean's body.

A, because the woman was standing to his right. And B, because Sean didn't let go of my wrist, forcing me to walk one way only.

"Hello," I said with false cheer. "Who are you?"

The woman, a blonde in her mid-thirties, stared at me with annoyance on her face.

"I'm Falon."

I blinked.

"I'm Naomi, nice to meet you!"

The false cheer in my voice had Sean drawing me into his chest, his hand squeezing my hip tightly.

"You're the bitch that took twenty minutes in the bathroom."

I looked at her.

"Yep, that's me."

She narrowed her eyes. "You're a fucking bitch."

"That's enough," Sean said. "Was there a reason that you're talking to me?"

Falon took in my face and body, lingering slightly on where Sean's hands were wrapped around my hip, and she curled a lip up at me.

"I…"

"Woman, don't you know when to quit?" a big biker walked up to her side, wrapped one beefy hand around her upper arm, and pulled her away.

All the while she bitched at the man.

"That was fun," I chirped.

Sean looked down at me.

"You didn't spend twenty minutes in the bathroom. More like eight," he rumbled.

My mouth twitched.

"I like you," I blurted.

His eyes took in my face. My eyes. My hair that was still in a mess at the top of my head, and grinned.

"That's fuckin' awesome, because I like you, too," he hesitated, bending down low so I could hear exactly what he had to say without all the ears surrounding us listening in. "And I plan to show you all the ways that I like you if you'll let me."

Before I could reply, he leaned back, captured my hand, and led us back over to where the Dixie Wardens were huddled in a circle, talking about this year's election.

***

Three and a half hours later I had a belly full of smoked meat, water, and cheesecake.

I'd changed my bag, used the restroom once more, and was sitting on the back of Sean's bike, waiting for him to join me.

I was sitting there talking to Imogen next to me when the drunk biker, who was even drunker now, stumbled toward his bike.

BB had a black eye, a bruised cheek, nose, and chin. The entire side of his face looked like he'd rubbed himself down in black war paint.

I knew better, though.

It was a bruise from Sean's fist hitting his face.

Wincing, I returned my eyes back to Imogen, dismissing him almost before he'd registered on my brain.

The less attention he received, the less power he had over the situation.

"My ass hurts already," Imogen groaned. "I don't know how they turned a usual thirty-minute ride into a three-hour ride."

"All I hear is bitch, bitch, bitch," Aaron teased as he walked up, Sean at his side. "Would it kill you to say something positive for once?"

Imogen's lips twitched as her eyes narrowed.

"No, probably not," she said teasingly. "Is this kind of like giving positive reinforcement instead of negative?" She tapped her lip with her finger.

"Kind of like saying, 'you performed oral sex well, and you have quite a bit of skill at kissing', instead of saying 'you have a small wiener and I can't feel it when it's inside of me?'"

Sean, Aaron, and Imogen looked at me like I'd shocked them.

"What?"

Imogen burst out into peals of giggles, while Sean rolled his eyes and handed me my helmet. "Helmet up, girl."

I did, a small smile on my face as I did.

By the time I had it situated and my hair tucked underneath it, as good as I could get it, Sean was in place in front of me, his hard ass sucked in tight to the inside of my thighs.

We were one of the lasts to take off while Sean waited for Aaron, who also waited for his wife to get her giggles under control.

And by the time we took off, we were one of five left in the parking lot.

Big Papa, Tommy Tom, and Jessie James had already eased out onto the road, fully expecting us to catch up.

And we did.

CHAPTER 7

A good thing about water is that you can drink it at work. A good thing about Vodka is that it looks like water.
-Sean's secret thoughts

Sean

We would have stayed caught up, too, had another biker that was one of three on our ass, trying to catch up like the rest of us, not lost control and run head first into a guardrail.

My immediate reaction was to stop, but pieces of the man's bike were flying everywhere.

Debris exploded, the majority of the bike vaulted down the guardrail, and it took everything I had not to wreck myself.

I knew Naomi was scared.

I was bobbing, weaving, and sliding my way like Aaron was beside me.

Naomi's hands tightened on my waist, and I felt her head curl in low on my back as she pasted herself to my body.

Good girl, I thought.

The bike slowed as I maneuvered around a tailpipe and the

handlebars, wrapped around each other like they'd always been so, and I finally placed my feet on the ground near the edge of the road.

Aaron followed suit beside me.

I looked at him, trying to get my heartrate under control, and stared.

He was just as shaken as me. Imogen was plastered to his back much like Naomi was to mine.

"My God," Naomi breathed, then scrambled off of the bike behind me.

I followed suit and started running, even though I knew what I'd see.

Pieces of the man's bike were everywhere.

And so was blood.

And other things.

"Fuck," I hissed.

The 'other things' were what worried me. That could've just as easily been me.

I'd seen the oil slick on the road. I'd avoided it, just like Aaron had. But, just like everything else, it was the luck of the draw.

But worrying did me no good, so I boxed it up and compartmentalized it, instead focusing on the fact that there was an emergency scene in front of me, and we were on a blind curve that offered almost zero visibility until you'd already partially rounded the curve.

"Aaron, head on up there and…"

He was already on it, moving up the street at a jog.

Trusting my brother, I turned to find Naomi dropping down to a knee beside what was the biggest part of what was left of the body

And there sadly wasn't much.

"Dead," she murmured as I approached.

"Oh, my God! Wood!" a woman cried, jumping off of another bike and running toward the scene.

Another biker caught her, one from another unofficial club, Hail House, and kept her from moving into the debris.

He looked at me and I shook my head.

"Wounds incompatible with life," I murmured, filling in the blank.

His face looked ravaged.

It was then I saw the cut, laying by itself, in the middle of the road.

How it'd gotten off, I didn't know. Accidents were so unpredictable, though.

Panic and adrenaline were a dangerous combination for a motorcycle driver. Even the most experienced rider might do things that they wouldn't have normally done. Or they might not do something that they would have, such as avoiding the pieces of wreckage like I'd done.

Sirens sounded in the distance, along with motorcycle pipes.

I knew who was coming back before I had visual proof.

My father had a sixth sense when it came to me. He always had.

When I was in trouble, he would know.

One time in high school, I'd gotten the grand idea to go joyriding in my father's '69 Mustang. It was a lot of power in a small package, and of course, being the dumb sixteen-year-old I'd been, I'd thought I could handle it.

Turned out that I couldn't, and I'd wrecked it spectacularly.

My father had felt that something was wrong and was already headed in my direction.

He showed up in time to help me out of the car.

And about a minute and a half later, the car blew up.

Then the cops showed.

If he not shown up when he had, my father would've lost his son.

And I felt terrible.

Now, watching him wind the curve, I realized that he was just as worried now as he was back then, almost twenty odd years ago.

His face took in the wreckage, and I saw the moment that terrible feeling crossed his face. He thought it was me who crashed.

I stood up from the crouching position I had been in when I was checking the man's vest, and I immediately waved at my father.

His eyes snapped to me, and I actually saw the relief come over him.

Tommy Tom was the next one to round the curve, followed shortly by Jessie James and Fender.

Jessie James looked just as relieved to see me as my father, and I wondered why.

"Should we do anything else?" Naomi captured my attention.

I looked down at her, studied her pale face, and shook my head.

"No. Nothing we can do at this point," I murmured. "If we were at home and in the medic, I'd have more things I could do, but since this isn't my area, and we're not working, my hands are tied."

She nodded once and started moving toward Imogen, who was trying hard to hold it together.

Her eyes kept straying to what used to be the man's body, and I grimaced.

I captured Naomi's hand and urged her to follow me.

Once we made it to Imogen, I captured her hand as well, and pulled both women securely into the circle of my arms.

"Do you think Aaron will kill me for hugging his girl?" I rumbled, trying to capture Imogen's attention.

"No," Imogen sniffled, sounding relieved. "As long as your hands stay above the waist, I'm sure he'll be good."

I grinned. "Duly noted."

"Sean."

I looked up to find my father barreling down on me.

Before I could let the women go, my father had his hulking arms around all three of us, pulling us into his big, barrel chest and shaking with pent up emotion.

"I'm okay, Pop."

Dad only hugged us tighter.

With nothing else to do, my eyes scanned the area, and I winced when I saw the biker I'd almost thrown down with, standing beside what had to be his bike, watching on with a blank expression on his face.

Where I'd thought that the drunk was walking to the cab that had pulled up in front of the smokehouse, he'd actually gone to his bike.

He was extremely lucky that it wasn't him who had died.

Because, even now, his whole body was swaying.

His eyes moved from the wreckage, and I saw the moment he realized I was looking at him.

His eyes narrowed and his fists clenched.

His gaze moved to the woman on my right, Naomi, and I saw them narrow even further.

I disentangled myself from my father, allowing the women to stay, and then moved so my body protected Naomi's from the man's cruel gaze.

I didn't like him one bit.

I'd walked up about thirty seconds before Naomi had made it into the bathroom, and I'd seen him harassing her. Saw him reach for her hair and her disentangle herself from him.

I also saw him step toward the door, come to a decision, then head to the men's room.

I'd then stopped and waited to go to the bathroom even though I hadn't really had to go.

I'd hoped the man would hurry, but he hadn't, instead taking just as long as Naomi had.

The door had opened about thirty seconds before hers, and I'd decided to use the facilities while I'd been standing there, thinking that Naomi would be a few minutes longer since I had been working with her over the weeks and knew that it took her longer than I'd been standing there to do what she had to do.

When I'd gone to pass the man into the bathroom, the man had moved and refused to allow me entry.

He'd then told me to stay away from the blonde girl, as if it were him who had come with her on the back of his bike instead of me.

I'd, of course, caused the man to stiffen by using a few choice words and it'd deteriorated from there.

And then Naomi had come out of the door of her own bathroom, causing me to react before I'd thought.

"You okay?"

I turned to find Imogen staring at me, her eyes on me instead of the wreck behind us.

Police finally showed on the scene, but I kept my eyes on my club member's old lady.

"Yeah," I replied gruffly. "Fine."

She looked like she didn't believe me, but she chose not to call me on it.

"Are your bikes blocked in?"

That came from Naomi, who was watching me with worry on her face as more and more police showed, followed by the volunteer firefighters.

"Nah," I said. "Dad, why don't you come help me move them before they really do get blocked in."

Dad let the women go, and then gestured to Tommy Tom with a jerk of his chin.

"Go over there, girls."

The 'girls' obeyed, crowding in close to Tommy Tom, who was watching the scene with grim understanding.

Dad followed me to the bikes, and we moved them quickly out of the way.

"Scared the shit out of me again," Dad finally said.

I turned to him as I flipped the stand back down on my bike next to where the rest of our group was standing.

"I know," I said quietly. "Scared the shit out of myself."

Dad's lips twitched.

Minutes passed and turned into hours.

I held Naomi in my arms, felt her shiver with the memories of the last few hours once again, and I squeezed her tight in my arms for what felt like forever.

We were questioned. Questioned again. Asked to move. And then asked to leave.

And through it all, she stayed in my arms, seemingly content to be there.

It was nearing twilight when I finally pulled up in front of my house with the rest of our group.

"I don't want to go home," she murmured over my shoulder to me.

Today had been bad. I didn't want to spend the night alone, either.

The bad wrecks always got to me like that, though. Never before had I had someone to lean on, though. Someone to ask to stay.

Hence the reason I invited her to stay at my place.

"Then stay with me."

She blinked.

"I left my house unlocked, and I don't have any clothes," she hedged.

I grinned.

"I know the way back to your house," I told her. "And I also know that I have room in my saddle bag for a few changes of clothing."

Her eyes widened.

"I know you have to go to work tomorrow night," I explained. "You can change your clothes into your daily wear, and then put your uniform on that night. That way you won't have to go all the way back home just to change."

She stared at me for a few moments, then nodded once. "I think I'd like that."

CHAPTER 8

Home is where I can stand in the kitchen, naked while eating peanut butter, and rapping an old-school Ludacris song and not be judged.
-Text from Naomi to Sean

Naomi

"I didn't realize that you lived in a trailer," I murmured as I walked in the door of Sean's RV after running by my house for an overnight bag.

Well, if that was what one would call it.

"It's an Airstream," he informed me. "What's cool about it is that it's made out of old jet materials."

"What?"

"During World War Two, the government forced the manufacturer of the Airstream to shut down production because the aluminum that was being used to make them was in such high demand. Hence the 'jet materials' comment," he explained as he started flipping on lights.

I didn't know what I was expecting, but it certainly wasn't what I saw.

"It looks like a mini apartment on wheels," I breathed. "This is beautiful."

Sean dropped his keys onto the table that was poking out of the corner of the room, and I followed suit with my own purse and keys.

The interior of the trailer was pleasant. Almost as if it were done with the intent to sell it. The easiest and most pleasant to appeal to both men and women.

"Did you redo this?" I asked.

I eyed the dome shaped walls and roof that were lined with aluminum. The couches were nice. A nice warm brown leather that looked like they'd accept me as a part of it if I sat down right now.

Then there was the sink. A full farm house sink took up what minimal countertop that there was, with one of the largest faucets I'd ever seen.

The stainless-steel countertops were even cooler, rounding out the whole industrial look perfectly.

The sight of Sean's bed, though…that was where I wanted to be.

I wanted to lie down on that white down comforter, bury my head under his pillows, and never get back up again.

"Take a shower first," Sean said, practically reading my mind. "Wash the dirt of the road off your skin. I like my bed clean."

I turned and stuck my tongue out at him.

"You're an ass," I said, but sat down on the kitchen chair that was one of two next to a postage stamp sized dining room table. "But I like you anyway."

Sean moved to the kitchen sink, washed his hands, and then dried it on a towel that said 'I like Big Tits.'

"Nice towel," I observed dryly. "Where can I get one for myself?"

He grinned. "My best friend from high school got it for me. He has a quirky sense of humor."

I could imagine.

Though, I really did like the towel. I had a few shirts that were vulgar.

Like the one I brought to change in to.

"What's for dinner?" I asked as I slipped my first boot off.

He opened the fridge and grabbed a beer, twisting the top off of and tossing the lid in the sink. All the while he kept his eyes on the fridge as he examined its contents.

"I can grill some chicken. Fry some chicken. Or we can have sandwiches."

Fried chicken sounded amazing.

"What do you feel like doing?" I questioned.

He looked at me.

"I don't care, to be honest," he admitted. "The easiest thing is sandwiches, but I'm starving, and I'd have to have four at this point to fill me up."

My mouth twitched.

"Chicken."

He rolled his eyes and sighed. "I knew you were going to pick that. Knew it!"

I shrugged. "I'm hungry. And honestly, I had a sandwich for breakfast."

"Okay," I said. "I'll help you cut the fat off the chicken if we can have mashed potatoes."

He smiled that smile that could bring me to my knees. "I can do that."

I took a quick shower, changed into clean clothes, and we worked in his tiny kitchen, brushing up against each other as we moved about.

By the time dinner was on the small kitchen table, my heart was pounding, my cheeks were flushed, my panties were drenched, and I wondered if I could go where this was going.

I hadn't had sex for a long time. At least two years, if not more.

But that wasn't even the scariest part.

My body wasn't the same as it used to be. I wasn't just a girl who was insecure about her body. Now I was an insecure woman who knew with certainty that her body wasn't attractive.

I mean, who would find a colostomy bag attractive? I wouldn't...

"Hey," Sean's deep voice broke into my thoughts. "What's that look on your face for?"

Like I would tell him the truth.

Oh, nothing much. I want to fuck you, but I'm not sure how you'll react to having my poop bag squished between us while we're doing the dirty.

Instead I said, "I'm starving."

"Then why aren't you eating?" he challenged.

I picked up my fork and knife and cut it all into bite sized pieces before I started to dig in.

It wasn't until I was four moans into my fourth bite when I realized that Sean wasn't eating.

I looked up at him, fork suspended in the air, and raised my brows at him.

"What?" I asked, taking in the strange look on his face.

"Good?" he sounded slightly strangled.

I nodded, not answering.

He carefully picked up his fork, speared a bite, and then popped it into his mouth.

He didn't moan, and I wondered if he had enough gravy. I eyed his plate, seeing his large knife resting against the side of the plate, and returned my attention to Sean's eyes.

"I think you need more gravy."

He looked at me like I was just on this side of crazy.

"I have a lot of gravy," he pointed to the overflowing gravy that was on his mashed potatoes.

"But you have none on your fried chicken. It's sacrilege."

I indicated this by showing him my plate. What I had resembled soup with globs of mashed potatoes and chunks of fried chicken rather than a plate of food dressed with some gravy.

He curled his lip up at me.

"I think I'm good," his lips twitched.

I shrugged and continued to scoop the food into my mouth, wondering if I looked like a fat ass with how much I was eating and how fast I was shoveling it in.

Then I decided not to care.

If he couldn't handle this about me, then we'd never work together. I was a girl who liked to eat. Tacos, fried chicken, gravy, rolls and macaroni and cheese were my all-time favorites. If those five things were in the same room as me, they were going to be eaten. I couldn't help myself.

I was nearly to the end of my meal when I realized, once again, that Sean hadn't eaten nearly as much as I had.

I took one last fork full of food and pushed the plate slightly away.

I would've pushed it further away if there was room to do that, but if I pushed it much more, it would move Sean's plate closer to him. And with the way he was looking at me, I wasn't sure what was wrong with him.

Not wanting to set him off, I watched him staring at me.

It took him a few long minutes, but he finally said something.

"I like that you like my food."

I blinked, surprised by that.

"Okay," I said. "It was *really* good."

He grinned. "I got that by all the moaning and groaning you were doing. It's like you were having sex…with the food I cooked you," he hesitated. "I want to hear those same sounds coming out of your mouth while my cock is inside of you."

Should I tell him that I wanted that, too? Should I tell him that I'm scared shitless that he'll see me as disgusting when I take my shirt off? Would he notice if I left my shirt on? Or maybe he could take me from behind.

"When you go quiet like this, it drives me fucking insane. I want to know what you're thinking."

His rumbled words had me bringing my eyes—eyes that I hadn't even realized that I'd dropped away from his—back up his assessing gaze.

I chose to run into the bathroom and close the door, composing my thoughts.

Once I'd checked my bag, and washed up, I headed back out to the bedroom where I found him staring at me expectantly.

"You scare me," I informed him. "I want you to like me. I want you to want me. I want you to swear to me that you'll never hurt me. But most of all, I want you to take me with that promise in your eyes that I'll enjoy the shit out of it and you won't let me down."

I wasn't immediately aware of how much of an invitation it sounded like until I was being hauled up by my armpits and then shoved onto the bed.

My back hit the white duvet cover, I bounced and then I found myself without pants.

My shoes had come off with the force of my pants leaving my body, and before I could do anything, even scream, I found myself flipped over onto my belly, my hips brought to the edge of the bed, and my panties following the same direction as my pants had taken only moments before.

I gasped, and went up on my elbows as I tried to brace myself, but I forgot how to breathe when I felt his lips on the inside of my thighs.

"I've wanted to fuck you since I saw you the first day you were on shift with me," he growled. "Wanted to taste you. Touch you. Have you. Now I've got you in my bed, and I can't figure out what I want to do first."

I breathed out shakily.

"To smell your sweet scent with my mouth only inches from your hot," he ran his tongue up the inside of my thigh. "Sweet," the other thigh. "Pussy."

He ran his tongue through the seam of my sex, and I moaned, reaching forward to grab the pillow that was at the top of the bed.

The minute I had it in my hand, I buried my face into it, wondering if I was too loud and if someone would hear.

But then he licked me again, and I felt the rasp of his beard on the inside of my thighs, and I forgot everything but what I was feeling.

The experience of him licking my most private place was almost surreal.

I couldn't believe this big, broad, sexy beast of a man with the most amazing beard I'd ever seen in my life actually wanted me.

ME! The woman who was always second best. The woman who was often cheated on, who was never really wanted by anyone in the first place.

But when he growled into my pussy, pressing his face even deeper into me while he licked me from behind, I realized something.

This man wanted me, really wanted me.

He wanted my pussy.

And I was giving it to him.

I might regret it in the morning, or might not, but for right now— this man was mine.

And I wanted his cock inside of me.

"Inside, please. I need you inside. Your cock."

My words were broken and stilted, but it was because I couldn't figure out how to speak clearly. My brain was mush.

He laughed.

But did he give me what I asked? *No. Not exactly.*

What he did give me was his fingers along with his mouth.

One hand went to one ass cheek and pulled it, allowing himself more room while the other hand snaked up the outside of my thigh and moved in, one blunt finger trailing along the lips of my sex.

The moment he was poised at my entrance, I shivered in anticipation.

"You want this?"

I nodded, my hair coming loose from my messy bun.

"Yes," I pleaded. "Please."

He pressed that finger to my entrance and breached me. Pressing so slowly inside that I had to fight not to push back against him.

But when I tried to do just that, his hand on my ass tightened and he said, "Don't move. I'm playing."

I wanted to cry out in frustration, but he didn't give me the chance.

Why?

Because he went from teasing me to rapid thrusts in a matter of moments.

No longer were his movements slow and taunting.

Now they were fast, hard, amazing.

It was exactly what I needed.

I opened my mouth and bit the pillow I was holding on to, crying out when his tongue went back to my clit.

I cursed and pushed back despite his orders, and bit the pillow to keep my cries of ecstasy inside.

He exhaled over my clit, and it was then I realized that he'd shifted so that now his head was now underneath me, and my hips were pulled away slightly from the bed to allow him room.

When had he done that?

Quickly, he recaptured my attention as he sucked my clit softly into his mouth, giving it a tentatively soft lick.

"Oh, fuck," I moaned.

His hand on my ass pushed up slightly, telling me without words that he wanted me to lift said leg.

And when I did, I was rewarded by his fingers sinking deeper inside of me.

Then they curled, tapping against my G-spot, and I lost all rational thoughts as an orgasm suddenly tore through me so freakin' fast that I hadn't even had time to brace.

Stars danced behind my closed eyelids, as wave after wave of elation poured through me.

I grunted as his fingers made one last thrust into me and then collapsed onto the bed, and incidentally onto his face.

It took me a few long seconds to realize what I'd done, but by the time I figured it out he was already wiggling out from under me.

"Oh, God," I moaned, looking at him over my shoulder as he came to a standing position behind me. "I'm so sorry."

His grin was one that clearly said he didn't care that I'd fallen onto his face at the peak of my passion. "Don't worry," he said as he ripped his shirt off over his shoulders and dropped it to the floor. "I didn't mind."

I continued to watch him, bringing my knees further up underneath me, and went to sit up onto my shins.

He stopped me with one huge hand on the small of my back. "Stay."

I did, waiting for what he would do next.

And what he did next was enough to send a shiver of fear through my body.

"Holy cow," I breathed as he ripped his pants open, one button at a time, and then shoved them and his underwear down to his knees.

I licked my lips as I got my first good look at his cock, and I wondered if it was possible to take something that large into an orifice so small.

Surely his cock wasn't as big as it seemed.

Something sounded in the yard beyond the trailer, and my eyes widened as I realized what I was hearing.

"Is that your dad?"

An hour or so before when we'd arrived, I was surprised to find that behind the house we'd been in earlier was a trailer. *In the driveway.* It was right next to where the men parked their bikes when we'd arrived back home.

But now, I could hear a motorcycle starting up right outside the window.

Son. Of. A. Bitch.

"No idea," the man that was running his work-roughened hand down the ridge of my spine murmured.

Then I felt what resembled a steel pole covered in flesh bump up against the inside of my thigh, and stiffened.

"Sean," I pleaded. "We can't."

Then he pressed that hard cock of his up against my entrance, started to push inside, and then cursed and backed away.

I looked behind me as he stomped away, stopping in front of a cabinet that was just to the right of the kitchen area.

He pulled the cabinet open, yanked down a box that was clearly a package of condoms—one, might I add, that had a layer of dust on it—and viciously ripped into it.

The way he was tearing into it actually made me smile, but the moment he turned and I got another look at his big cock, nerves started to ripple in my belly.

"Have you ever permanently scarred a woman when you were taking her?" I asked as he made his way back to me, a condom in his hand.

He didn't answer, instead held the package with his teeth and pulled out the contraceptive, and then tossed the wrapper in the vicinity of the sink.

My eyes went to his hands as I watched in fascination while he slicked it down his cock.

"It's red," I murmured.

"And ribbed," he agreed.

I opened my mouth to say something more, and then shut it when I heard the motorcycle rev up, and then descend down the driveway.

Relief must've shown on my face, because Sean grinned.

"Been doing this for five years now, darlin'," he informed me. "Dad knows better by now."

I didn't believe him.

"You can't be positive."

He came back up behind me and I dropped my head back down to my pillow, squeezing my eyes shut tightly as I waited for him to enter me.

"If the trailer's rockin'," he rumbled. "Dad doesn't come a' knockin'."

With that he pushed into me, spearing me with his big, hard cock.

I screamed.

Both in a good and a bad way.

I'd never, not once, felt so full as I did right then.

I'd had five sexual partners in my life and none of them had been as big, or as thick, as Sean was.

He touched me in places that I never knew were even there to be touched, and kept touching.

As more and more of him filled me, I felt his hips hitting the back of my legs, and I was fairly certain that if I died today, I would die a very happy, fulfilled woman.

He hadn't even started to really move yet, and I was already on the verge of coming again.

His hands clenched on my hips, as I breathed in through my nose and out through my mouth in an effort to gain control of the situation.

But Sean didn't want me in control. He didn't want me to be anything but aware of him. Which I was.

Very much so.

"Sean," I whimpered. "Please."

I didn't even know what I was asking for at this point. *To fuck me? Pull out? Rub my clit?*

He was obviously aware of what I needed, though, because he withdrew and then slowly filled me back up.

He did this for over and over while I tried to catch my breath.

It took me a few long moments of pulling air into my lungs to realize that it was futile.

I wasn't going to catch my breath.

Not with Sean's magnificent cock inside of me, and sure as hell not while his hands were clenching so tightly on my hips that it was almost painful.

He never let up, he just kept stroking into me, over and over again, as I tried not to scream so loud that Sean's ears would hurt.

"You want my hand, baby?" Sean asked as he paused in his ministrations.

I moaned into my pillow, and bucked back against him, wondering if he was going to smack my ass for participating.

"Sit still," he ordered, not with a smack to my ass, but with two hard squeezes on my hips that told me to stay exactly as he had me positioned.

I would have bruises the shape of his fingertips on my hips in the morning.

I didn't care, though.

Nope, not one single bit.

What I did care about was coming, and I knew that I would if I just got him to speed up…or thrust harder.

"Please," I repeated my earlier plea. "I'm so close."

Sean's mouth moved to my shoulder blade, and one hand went into my hair at the base of my neck.

"Sit up," he ordered. "Now."

I did, wondering what he would do if I refused.

And I found out because, apparently, I didn't hustle quickly enough at his command.

Mostly because he fisted his hand into my hair and pulled me up, causing me to pause for a second as a shiver of anticipation skated up my spine.

"Sean," I breathed out shakily. "You're driving me crazy."

He laughed in my ear, letting his mouth run along the delicate skin of my neck.

"I drive you crazy?" he asked. "How do you think I feel?" He bit down lightly on the skin at the base of my neck. "I tried to take this slow, but your pussy is so fucking tight, and you're squeezing those muscles every few seconds, trying my patience and my sanity."

I squeezed involuntarily, and he groaned into my ear.

"I've wanted you for weeks. Then, today, you rode on the back of my bike, wrapped around me, for hours, sometimes with your hand in my lap, laying right over my goddamned cock. And you wonder why I have no fucking patience?"

I didn't wonder at all, actually.

What I was thinking about, however, was the way this new position made him feel inside of me.

I felt him everywhere.

"Touch yourself," he ordered.

My eyes fell closed, and I moved my hand down to come to a rest on my pubic bone. My fingers were curled lightly around the lips of my sex, and I moved one lone finger through the folds, amazed by how wet I was down there.

Then I came into contact where his cock was moving inside of me, and my heart started to pick up.

I was so stretched, that it felt like my entrance was straining to accommodate him. I knew if he wasn't careful, he really could hurt me.

But I didn't need to worry.

The man knew what he was doing, that was for sure.

Especially when he started to lift me, his large hand around my waist. Moving me up and down the length of his shaft, filling me over and over in smooth, calculated thrusts.

"Goddamn, you feel like fuckin' heaven," he rumbled, his beard tickling my shoulder. "I keep thinking I'm going to be able to hold on for you to come, and then I get to thinking about how good you feel and forget I'm supposed to wait."

I curled my arm up and around his neck, holding his head to me as I turned my own and pressed a soft, wet kiss on his lips.

He growled into my mouth, and suddenly I found myself empty, crying out, and flipping to my back.

He was on me before I could comment on his abruptness, filling me back up with his length, and hitting new and even more exciting spots inside of me.

The breath left me once again, the third, fourth, or whoever knew how many times, and I struggled not to pass out from the pleasure he was inflicting on me.

I lifted my feet, curling them around his big body, and held on as he took me roughly.

"Fuckin' get there," he growled. "Or I'll go without you." He sounded tortured, but I didn't argue with his terse words.

Instead, I moved my hand back in place, and slowly started to circle my clit, being careful not to touch where we were joined again.

Because despite what most women said, I did want to get off. I wanted to come with him inside of me, and it did matter if he came and I didn't.

In the end it didn't matter, because all it took was eight circles of my fingers, combined with his precise thrusts hitting that special spot inside of me that no one else had ever hit before in my life, and I was coming.

Hard.

I clamped down so hard on him that I knew the instant he knew I was coming.

His eyes changed, his jaw clenched, and he stared into my eyes as he let go, too.

We came together.

Him only seconds behind me.

And it. Was. Glorious.

At least until he collapsed beside me, his large, muscular arm going over my chest, and his thick, strong thigh pinning down one leg.

"Ughhh!" I groaned. "You weigh a freakin' ton, Sean."

He didn't move.

"Seanshine!"

He got up on one elbow and narrowed his eyes at me. "Don't call me that."

My lips twitched, but my eyes, I hoped, remained innocent.

"Why not?" I asked joyfully, running my bare foot up and down the length of his thigh. "I think it's cute."

He bent down and bit my lip lightly.

"Because I asked you not to," he tried.

I shook my head, grinned, and said, "Not good enough."

He growled and pulled back, his cock sliding out of me.

Then his fingers were there, touching me and feeling me, and I blushed.

"What are you doing?" I demanded, sitting up.

He let his fingers slide through my folds to my entrance, and probed softly.

"Just making sure I didn't do any irreparable damage," he teased.

I picked up the pillow I'd screamed in the entire time, and hit him upside the head with it.

"Shut up." I pushed him away and stood up, walking carefully to the bathroom.

I was sore, but it was a good kind of sore. One where I would be feeling him tomorrow while I was at work. And remembering how good he felt inside of me the entire time, counting down the hours until we could do it again.

He whistled softly behind me, making me toss him a smile over my shoulder.

"Excuse me, while I clean up," I told him as I walked into his bathroom and closed the door.

I felt him moving about the RV, likely discarding the used condom, and looked at myself in the mirror.

I didn't look any different.

Sure, my neck was beard burned, and my face was awash with color, but it wasn't that different than my usual.

And the funny thing was, was that I felt good.

Definitely not nervous like I thought I'd be, or embarrassed.

I didn't once think about my colostomy bag until I sat on the toilet to clean myself.

During when he had me up on my knees, my back to his front, he had to have felt it. It was nearly impossible not to notice.

But he hadn't said a word. He didn't make a big deal of it, and he didn't seem to really even care.

And that made me...*happy*. Exceptionally happy.

I liked that he didn't make a big fuss about it. At least not the way my brother had when he'd first seen it.

The icing on the cake, though? That was knowing that the man I'd slowly been falling for the last few weeks had the hots for me just like I had the hots for him.

Yes, it was good to be Naomi Beth Dwyer. Very, very good.

CHAPTER 9

I don't need fun to have alcohol.

-Fact of life

Naomi

It was bad to be me.

Very, very bad.

Especially right then.

"Hi," I said, embarrassment flooding my cheeks as I walked down the steps of Sean's camper.

Big Papa looked up at me, took one look at my attire, and grinned.

"Morning, girl," he rumbled, clearly amused by my embarrassment.

I waved, then hurried to my car that a prospect had so nicely brought over for me, which happened to be directly next to the motorcycle that Big Papa was mounting.

He was dressed in his police uniform, and he had a revolver at his hip that was about half as long as his leg. His hair was unkempt, and he had a helmet in his hand that he was lifting to fit onto his head.

"Have a safe day," I called, opening my car door.

Big Papa's lips twitched. "You too, girl."

I shivered, knowing that I would never hear the end of this, and dropped down into my car seat, wondering if it was too early to call my best friend.

I checked my watch, bit my lip, and then shrugged.

I didn't really care if it was too early. Four forty-five wasn't that early, and I needed to talk to Aspen about as bad as I needed to get to work.

Looking at my watch as I started my car, I came to a decision.

Pulling out my phone, I dialed the number that I had been calling since I was in high school when we both got our new phones, and placed it to my ear.

Aspen answered on the first ring.

"Where have you been?" she hissed, sounding angry.

I grinned.

"Good morning to you, too," I said cheerfully. "How are you and the fam?"

Aspen didn't waste time. She only demanded answers.

"I've dealt with my brother going to the ER because they think he has appendicitis, and I've been trying to get a hold of you for going on six hours now."

It was going on nine hours, but I wasn't going to correct her. She sounded like shit.

"Is your brother okay?" I asked, worry filling my tone.

"Yes," she sighed. "It was only gas."

I covered my mouth, trying really hard not to laugh.

Unfortunately, I wasn't successful.

The motorcycle at my side roared to life, and I looked just as Big Papa started to walk his way backward down his driveway. Once he reached the end, he pushed something with his foot, and then the big man shot forward down the road, not caring if he woke the entire neighborhood up with the loud beast.

"What was that?"

I sighed, put my car into reverse, and then backed down the driveway, too.

"That," I said as I watched my rearview mirror as I went, "was the father of Sean."

"You're sleeping with an old man?" Aspen gasped. "Please, tell me you at least used a condom. Gross. There's no telling where his old cock has been."

I put the car into drive, and just barely missed another motorcycle that was sitting on the side of the road two houses down from Sean's.

"Shit," I cursed, swerving slightly.

I hadn't seen the thing at all. *Jesus, that was close.*

And there was a man on it! Fuck!

I waved at the man, who did happen to be sitting on a black motorcycle in the dark night, while also wearing black himself. Jesus, was he asking to be ran over?

"Seriously," Aspen continued to rant. "You're a pretty woman. There's no reason in the world that you should be fucking old men."

"Aspen, I have to be up in less than an hour. For the love of God, shut the hell up."

I heard what sounded like covers rustling, and then the sound of her getting up and walking away from where I assumed she'd been in bed.

I smiled, thinking about her husband, Drew.

I'd been at the fire department with him for my entire paramedic career, and I actually missed him, even though he was older himself.

"You're one to talk," I said. "Your husband is old."

"He is not," she snapped.

It was an old argument, but one that I loved to rile her up about.

"And anyway, I'm not sleeping with an old man. I'm sleeping with a man older than me, but not by a whole lot. About a few years at most."

I didn't actually know his age, but I assumed he was about thirty-four to thirty-six years old. He didn't look much older than that.

"Hmm," Aspen hummed. "Is there a reason you couldn't tell me this last night when I called?"

"Because I was too busy having my vagina stuffed with a magnificent cock," I drawled.

Aspen gagged.

"Oh, you're one to talk. You never cease in telling me about Drew's magnificent cock. What's so different if I relay the same thing about the man that I'm sleeping with?" I asked, my eyes going to my rearview when I saw a single headlight pop up in it.

"Because I'm the one that is doing the telling…duh."

I turned onto the road that would lead me to my work, and wondered if I had time to stop and get coffee.

After a quick glance at the clock, I realized that I barely even had time to get to work, let alone stop for coffee.

"How's everyone doing?" I asked conversationally.

"Fine," she grumbled. "Drew picked up two forty-eight hour shifts this week, and will be gone Monday, Tuesday, Friday, Saturday."

That sucked.

"That sucks," I echoed my thoughts. "Why is he having to work two doubles?"

"Because PD's out with the flu," she answered hesitantly.

At one time, that would've worried me.

Now, not so much.

Not when I'd just left a hunky piece of man meat, happy and sated in his bed.

"That sucks," I repeated. "Glad I'm not there to catch that."

I was, too. I hated being sick. I was the type of woman that couldn't handle being sick. When I was sick with a cold, I couldn't function. There was something about being sick that really seemed to hit me hard and force me to slow down. It was almost as if my body knew I wouldn't take the time and rest, so it made me do it whether I wanted to do it or not.

Fuck responsibilities.

"Wow."

I started to break as I pulled into the station, waving at the paramedic I would be working with today.

I hadn't worked with him before, but he was handsome. Though, Sean had already warned me that he was an ass.

I would save my judgement until I knew better, though. I really didn't like to judge before I knew for a fact.

"Wow what?" I asked, reaching into the floorboard for my duffel of clothes that Sean had stopped at my house and allowed me to collect last night.

"I'm just surprised that you're not freakin' out, that's all," she amended. "It's nice to see that you're moving on. I was worried."

I was, too. Not that I would tell my friend that I had been.

There were certain things that she didn't need to know, and I wanted to keep it that way.

"Have you heard anything on my brother?" I asked, changing the subject.

My inadequacies were never a favorite topic of conversation for me.

The other end of the line was silent, and I started to get a sinking feeling in the pit of my stomach.

"Aspen."

She inhaled swiftly, then blew out the breath.

"He was arrested a few nights ago over a domestic disturbance with his former girlfriend."

My eyes closed.

A long time ago, I harbored hopes that my brother and Aspen would get married. Then he had to go and ruin it by cheating on her with his partner, a bitch of a cop that I despised.

Not because she was a bad cop, but because she was a nasty person. One that made my brother a bad person, too.

Danny, although a little selfish at times, wasn't a bad person before he got together with her. I didn't know this man that he'd turned into over the last year, and I hated that *that woman* had changed him for the worse.

"Why was he arrested?" I asked. "What happened?"

I heard what sounded like Aspen moving even further away from where she'd been previously standing. I then heard a door, likely the back door that led out onto her newly renovated deck, and then she began to speak, this time in a louder voice that I could actually hear.

"Apparently, there had been a big fight going on between the two for half the night before cops were actually called out," she started. "After the cops showed, Officer Slutface McWhorebag – who, I might add, has gotten pretty darn fat – accused Danny of hurting her. She showed the cops bruises and everything."

I closed my eyes.

"Jesus."

"Yeah," Aspen agreed quietly. "From what I've heard from my brother, Danny wasn't there the last two days, and the bruises are at least two days old if you go by the yellow coloring." She hesitated. "But his alibi is someone that he won't give up to Downy, so it's his word against hers at this point. Which, unfortunately, she's got a leg up on him in terms of reliability since he's still dealing with the backlash over running his own sister down with his police cruiser while he was drunk."

I winced.

"I'm okay," I said to her, reading the worry in her tone.

"I know you are, but I'm still freaked out," she said. "When I got that call, I was in the middle of watching a YouTube video on how to start an IV," she sniffled. "I was so scared for you."

My heart melted. "Ass, I have to start work. But I want you to know that I love you."

Aspen snicker-sniffled. "Don't call me ass. I love you, best friend."

My heart warmed even more. "I love you, too."

I got out of the car after she hung up, shouldering my duffel bag, and went inside.

The moment I crossed over the threshold, I had a broom thrust into my hand.

"Let's get this shit over with, so we can get on with the rest of our day," my partner said before turning on his heel and taking a seat at the bar where he pulled out one of those healthy meals that was separated into three small sections.

Every single shift, the station was to be mopped and swept, but not in that order. And if it got dirty throughout the day, we were also expected to give it a second cleaning if that was what we had to do.

However, normally that was the lower rank's, which would be an EMT, job. Since both Sean and I were the same rank of paramedic, it was assumed that we would just share the duty.

Apparently, my partner for the day didn't think that.

"I'll get right on that," I lied, pushing the broom's handle until it rested against the wall. "After I catch up on some sleep."

With that, I walked into the bedroom—the one that Sean slept in since my usual one with my locker was occupied by the douche, and fell right to sleep. The nice thing was, Sean's sheets smelled like him, and it was the best sleep I'd ever gotten while at the station.

***

By the time the shift was nearly over, I was about ready to kill Larry, my asshole partner, who thought we still lived in the sixteenth century.

Women couldn't do man's work. Such as lifting a patient.

Just one example of what an ass he'd been this day.

Sean (3:24 PM): How goes it?

I wanted to pull my hair out.

Naomi (3:24 PM): If I never see this man again, it'll be too soon.

Sean (3:25 PM): What'd he do? Want me to kick his ass?

My mouth twitched.

Naomi (3:26 PM): We were at a patient's house, and he asked the patient's son to help lift him onto the gurney because I was 'just a girl' with puny muscles.

Sean's typing showed on the screen, and it took him over two minutes to reply.

Sean (3:28 PM): When I worked with him, he assumed that I couldn't do my job. Tried to drive. Then told our boss once we were done on shift that he recommended I take a few hours of CE to re-examine what it was like to be 'nice to patients.'

I winced.

Naomi (3:30 PM): Did you kill him after that? Because that's seriously what I want to do.

Sean (3:34 PM): No. But I did write him up for leaving the ambulance unattended with the keys in it because he was a douche.

That was a big no-no.

The ambulance was a million-dollar machine when you added in all the equipment and drugs that were on board along with the cost of the ambulance itself. We were instructed from day one of orientation never to leave the rigs unattended, and if we witnessed it being done, then to report it.

Naomi (3:34 PM): I didn't know you were so petty.

I laughed as I said this, knowing that he wouldn't apologize at all.

"Do you think you'll get to the sweeping and mopping sometime today?" That was Larry, the loser.

I didn't bother looking up from my phone, instead focusing on deep breathing in order not to tell the man currently sitting next to me to fuck off and eat shit.

Luckily, my telephone rang, emitting a loud peel that made Larry the lazy jump.

Grinning inwardly, I put the phone to my ear.

"Hello?"

"Hi, Naomi. This is Dr. Corvey's office."

I blinked.

"Hello!" I said chipperly. "Is my appointment canceled?"

"No," the woman said. "We were just hoping you'd be willing to move it to this afternoon instead of tomorrow. Dr. Corvey has a conflict, and would like us to move all of tomorrow's appointments to today, if possible."

The door opened and I grinned, waving at my replacement.

"I can come right now," I informed her. "It'll take me fifteen minutes, max, to get there."

"That's wonderful. Be sure to have your insurance card with you," she ordered.

Promising I would, I waved at Melly, my replacement, and rushed out the door.

I arrived at my appointment an hour late, and left an hour and a half later with a surgery date for two days from then.

What did I do once I was done? Not call the man I should've called.

Instead, I went home, took a shower and started getting ready for surgery. Sean worked the next day and I didn't know if I should tell him I was having my colostomy reversal or if he would even be interested. I was busy with pre-surgery bowel preps and laxatives, but I got my duffel bag repacked with comfortable clothes and called my boss to arrange a few weeks off, but I still put actually calling Sean. He texted me often, but I put him off.

The next morning, I went into surgery, with no one in the waiting room waiting for me.

Lani Lynn Vale

CHAPTER 10

If you're willing to share your bacon with her, she might be the one.
-Dating tips

Naomi

One week later

"Now, I want you to take it easy, young lady," said the doctor who was my ticket out of the hospital after he'd completed my final exam before discharge. "If you have any unusual problems, please feel free to call my office, and my on-call staff will relay the information. If I think what you're experiencing warrants further examination, I'll likely send you straight back to the ER, okay?"

I nodded emphatically.

"Keep taking the stool softeners. Don't be surprised if you're in the bathroom for long periods of time, or if you find that you need to go urgently or frequently," he continued. "Also, make sure that you don't strain. A little blood in the stool is normal, a lot of blood in your stool means you need to call. If at any time something doesn't seem right, call. Okay?"

I nodded once more.

He grinned at me. "I'm glad I got back in time to release you."

I was, too.

The doctor, I'd realized during the appointment to schedule my reversal, was a nice guy. He was a part of the national guard, and went once a month to do his duties. He said he loved being in the military, so he didn't mind the continued commitment. He had spent part of this past week at the Alabama National Guard in Montgomery.

All of my x-rays and scans had come back great. I had healed better than they expected. So I'd taken him up on the offer of the reversal.

In that weeks time, I'd had a bad go of it.

I'd found out that I was allergic to two medications. I also found out that pooping wasn't the same as it used to be.

Something that came as a surprise, even though I'd been warned beforehand by the doctor.

"All right, then," Dr. Corvey said as he stood up from his stool. "I'll get the nurse to bring you your release papers."

With that, he left, leaving me wondering just how I was going to get home.

Being in a city that I didn't know, I didn't really have anyone to call—unless I called Sean.

Sean, who I hadn't informed I was having surgery, let alone spoken to since I'd had the surgery done, in well over a week.

He was probably not very happy with me.

But I'd made the decision, not because I thought Sean couldn't handle me having surgery, but because I didn't think he should have to.

We weren't anything. We'd had sex once, and I'd convinced

myself that he really wouldn't care.

Yes, I was that insecure.

Yet, deep down inside, I knew that wasn't true. He would've cared, but I'd taken the decision to have him at my side away from him, and I expected him to be a little upset by that.

"All right, Ms. Naomi. Your turn!" the nurse announced.

I clapped my hands excitedly, causing her to laugh.

I'd spent a week with these ladies on the floor, and every single one of them had clapped with me when they'd gotten the news that I was finally able to do number two...out of the *right* hole.

Now I knew that I would have a friend for life.

She'd even offered to let me borrow her cell phone charger when I'd realized I'd forgotten mine.

Though, that was rejected by me.

It was easier not knowing if Sean tried to call, instead of knowing that he hadn't.

"Ohhh," Abigail stopped me right outside the doorway of my room, and turned back. "I forgot these came for you while you were getting dressed."

She walked to the nurses' station and came back with a vase of flowers.

A really big vase with so many flowers in it that it was obvious that it'd cost a fortune.

"Thank you," I murmured. "Did they say who it was from?"

The meddling woman, the same one that'd been trying to get me to call Sean all week, grinned.

"The delivery guy said 'from your biker' to me. The card reads the same." She pointed at the card.

My belly warmed, and I closed my eyes, finally realizing just how stupid I'd been.

Maybe I should have called him. But then I realized that he had to know where I was to be able to send these. At least hours ago.

Why hadn't he come up here?

Sure, I was likely overreacting. In fact, I knew I was overreacting. Yet I didn't care. I wanted someone who freakin' cared. Who would show up, pissed as hell, that I had been missing a week without an explanation.

"Thanks," I said to her.

Abigail's face fell, and she pursed her lips. "I don't agree."

I knew she didn't.

I didn't know Abagail all that well, but in the short time I had her as my nurse, I knew she spoke her mind. Countless times she'd told me rather bluntly that this was real life. Shit happened, literally. So I needed to stop being embarrassed and live my life.

Something in which I'd promised her I'd do from now on. Something I felt that I could accomplish without that stupid colostomy bag weighing me down and preventing me from wearing the clothes that I wanted to wear.

"Damn, I forgot your prescriptions. Be right back."

She stopped me beside the elevator, next to an older man that I'd seen walking the floor right along with me over the last day that I'd been able to cajole my body up.

The man looked lost.

"Hello," I said, touching the old man on the shoulder. "Can I help you with something?"

He looked over at me in my own wheel chair, and shook his head.

He looked sad.

Really sad.

And I wanted to give the old man a hug.

I didn't usually do that. Now with strangers.

In my line of work, I saw a lot of men and women, especially older folks, who looked sad.

It seemed, the older you became, the lonelier you got. And this man, with his bushy white eyebrows, and his jowly face, looked lonelier than any I'd seen in a long time.

I didn't know what possessed me to talk to him, but I did.

"They're springing me. Are they springing you?"

His eyes returned to mine.

"I wasn't here because I was admitted. Just visiting the ladies who took care of my wife."

I blinked.

"Oh," I said, feeling embarrassed. "That's good, then. How's your wife doing?"

If I'd read his body language, I would've known that this was a sore subject, but I was trying to distract myself from the bouquet of flowers in my lap, instead focusing on this man who looked so sad.

"My wife died a little over six months ago," he rasped, his voice full of shakes. "She died, and these ladies on the floor did CPR on her for over an hour before the doctor called time of death. They make me feel closer to her, so I come up here and visit."

My stomach dropped.

If I'd been standing up, I would've swayed on my feet at the sound of the devastation in that man's voice.

"I'm sorry to hear that," I whispered, unsure what to say.

I was never good at finding the right thing to say. Which was why it was so hard for me to comfort patients' families. I was a paramedic, not a counselor, and at times I found it hard to say the right things when the right words were all you wanted to hear.

He shrugged, like it didn't bother him.

As long as you didn't look at his eyes, you might not know.

"Sorry, honey. Here they are." She handed them to me.

I looked at the filled prescriptions. "These are filled," I said dumbly.

Abigail snickered. "Technically, since you're an employee of the hospital through the ambulance service, you can fill your scripts at the hospital pharmacy at no extra cost to yourself."

That was awesome, though I didn't plan on being in a hospital anymore to use this convenience.

"Thank you," I smiled.

"Hello, Mr. Thorton. Are you on your way home?" Abigail asked, sounding surprised to see the man beside us.

"Hi, Abby Girl," he said thickly. "And I am."

"Did you ever find your dog?" she asked.

"No," he said. "She never came back home. I posted those fliers all over the neighborhood, but haven't heard a thing back on her."

Oh, God. The man had lost his dog, too? Only months after losing his wife?

That was freakin' horrible.

"I'm sorry to hear that, Mr. Thorton. How about you ride down with us, keep us company. This one gets to go home today after a week with us," she chattered along as if I wasn't even there. "I'm trying to convince her to call her man, but she's being stubborn. She called a taxi instead."

I bit my lip.

This woman, who'd been at my side and taking care of me for an entire week now, just didn't know how to shut up. She'd told everyone about my 'stupidity' as she called it.

"That who sent you those flowers?" Mr. Thorton glanced at the bouquet in my lap.

I looked down at the flowers, which wasn't far since the flowers were so big, and shook my head. "Yeah," I sighed. "They're from him."

"A man doesn't care, he wouldn't go to the trouble," he pointed out. "Looks to me that he cares."

The elevator doors opened, and I gripped my vase tightly as I saw the man I'd been doing my best to forget this last week standing there, waiting for the elevator doors to open.

He took one look at me, and he shuddered.

"About time," he rumbled. "Didn't think you'd ever get down here."

With that parting comment, he turned on his heels and started walking, not saying another word.

"He's hot," Abigail said. "You should really think about apologizing."

I narrowed my eyes at her, and she smiled.

"Just a thought."

I didn't want to hear her thoughts. In fact, all I wanted to do was admire the backside of Sean as he walked in front of us.

The moment he got to the truck, he opened the passenger side and waited for me to arrive.

Which didn't take long because Nurse Abby, the big busy-body butter-inner, had started pushing me faster and faster until she was practically power walking in the direction of Sean and his big ol' truck.

A truck that I was fairly certain I couldn't climb into at this point.

He must've realized this as I was rolled toward him, because the moment I was close enough, he started toward me.

"Do you walk?" I suddenly asked the man next to me, rolling only inches from my chair.

Abigail stopped in front of Sean, him only inches away from my knees, and put the brakes on the wheelchair.

I waved Sean off when he went to scoop me up.

"I want to."

He stepped back, letting his eyes trail over my face to gauge my determination.

Something must've registered on my face, however, because he stepped back once more, and turned his eyes to the man at my side.

I stood up, belly smarting as I did, and drew in a couple of deep breaths.

"Hello," Sean said, offering the old man his hand. "Thank you for keeping my girl company. She conveniently forgot to tell me that she was being let out today."

The old man smiled, and it transformed his face.

"Nice to meet you. Brady Thorton," Mr. Thorton answered, turning his attention to me. "I can walk...Why?"

I looked at the wheelchair.

He stood up, shakily might I add, and shuffled away from it a few steps.

My heart pounded in my throat.

Any time I saw someone, I automatically assessed them.

Mr. Thorton was old, but first and foremost, he was a fall risk. He had on shoes that looked like they were too big for his feet, and he had a bandage on his head.

"I mean, do you walk on any trails, like at a park or something," I amended, clearly seeing that he was proving a point to me. "I was told that I needed to walk to keep my, um, bowels moving. I just had a colostomy reversal, and they want me to exercise, not strenuously though, to help my, errrm, you know, move along."

The old man grinned. "I walk at the trail at Center and First every day." He stopped, then added. "It was what I was doing today when I fell and hit my head. Some guy's dog was off the leash and tripped me. I was on the floor before I even knew what happened."

I frowned. "There's a leash law in this city, right?"

That question was directed at Sean, and he nodded.

"There is," he confirmed. "Did you get the name of the dog owner?"

The old man shook his head. "I did not. I was too busy trying to staunch the blood flow."

My lips quirked.

"I'll meet you there tomorrow," I informed him.

He looked at me like I was crazy, like he didn't believe a word that was coming out of my mouth.

"We'll see."

With that, the old man walked away, and I was left with a man that had his arm around me, all the while Abigail watched with rapt fascination.

"Have a good day, lovely," Abigail said cheerfully. "Call me if you have any questions, or just want to talk."

On that note, she left me alone with Sean.

A man who I could tell was majorly pissed off that I hadn't called and told him I was being discharged. Or that I had been going into the hospital in the first place.

"How did you know that I was out?" I asked as I watched the old man shuffle to a waiting cab.

Sean sighed.

"Your friend called me. Told me that you got out at twelve, and that she suspected you'd try to take a cab," Sean said and reached for the door of his truck.

Abigail.

I knew that look on her face had been too innocent.

I'd listed Sean as my emergency contact. She obviously put the two 'Seans' together, otherwise she wouldn't have called my emergency contact.

Meddling woman.

To keep my eyes off the anger in Sean's eyes, I looked at the lifted truck, and wondered if I could hack it.

I didn't think that I could. My stomach wasn't hurting, per se, but it also didn't feel all that great, either.

Before I could tell Sean this, though, he bent down, scooped me up—one arm under my legs, and one behind my back—and placed me carefully in the passenger seat.

I blinked, surprised at how gentle he'd been, and realized he was really upset with me.

I sighed.

"I should've told you," I told him as he got into the car. "It was a surprise. I went to my doctor appointment, he told me he could fit me into the schedule two days later. I had a lot of prep work to do and I was busy getting ready to be gone for a few days."

He looked over at me, then turned back to the front and started the truck up.

"I realize that you're an independent woman who's used to taking care of herself, but it would've been nice to know that you were having surgery." He cleared his throat. "Even if we hadn't promised we'd be completely open with each other, I'd still tell you to pull your head out of your ass."

I started to snicker.

Forty minutes later, I was ensconced in Big Papa's house, in an old room that used to be Sean's, staring at the closed door in horror.

I'd really screwed this up.

I knew that within five minutes of being in the car with Sean.

He was mad.

So mad that he didn't say a word to me the entire ride to his place, even though I'd complained multiple times that I'd wanted to go home.

He'd ignored me, of course, and I'd been left sitting there fuming, wondering if a cab would even run as far out as they lived.

Probably not. I didn't have good luck.

Shit.

CHAPTER 11

*Parents these days can't control their kids in public. All my dad
had to do was look at me, and I got my shit together.
-Sean's words of wisdom*

Sean

Two hours later, I found myself walking back to my pop's house,
wondering if I was stupid or just crazy.

I was, obviously, looking forward to having my heart broken, that
much was for certain.

I still couldn't figure out what the hell I was doing.

My intention to leave her here and never speak to her again hadn't
worked as well as I'd planned.

In fact, the moment I heard laughter coming from my father's open
windows from the bed in my RV, I realized that maybe I hadn't
reached my peak limit of suffering today.

Which was why I found myself walking into my dad's place and
coming to a sudden halt.

There were a lot of people there.

My dad, Aaron and his wife. Tommy Tom and Tally. Verity and

Truth.

I could also vaguely hear Fender off somewhere in the back of the house talking on the phone to, who I assumed, was his baby mama.

The icing on the cake, however, was finding Jessie James with his arm running along the back of the couch, only inches from touching Naomi.

What, it wasn't enough that he had to steal one woman, now he had to take the other as well?

Fucking perfect.

"Hey, boy. You want a burger?"

I looked over at my pop after tearing my eyes away from Naomi, who was laughing at something Jessie had said.

"Nah," I said, clearing my throat when it didn't sound as strong as it seemed. "I just came to tell you I'm going to be gone for a few hours." I let my eyes trail back to the woman who was now staring at me, smile wiped from her face. "I have a few errands I need to run."

I was lying.

I didn't have any errands.

But I wasn't going to be responsible for what I did to Jessie if I stayed, which meant I *had* to go.

"Yo," Ghost said as he came up beside me. "You that busy?"

Ghost actually talking to me was new, at least lately.

He was different over these last couple of months.

Since the men in our tight knit group had started getting married and finding life partners, Ghost had become even more and more distant.

It'd started off gradually, and now, thinking back, I didn't remember when he'd disappeared almost completely.

But seeing him here at my father's place was the first time in, at least, three weeks.

He hadn't even ridden with us the smokehouse.

I couldn't remember the last time Ghost had missed a group ride.

Sure, he'd shown up eventually, but it'd only been after we'd arrived.

"No. Just a few errands that can wait. Why?" I asked.

His jaw worked. "I need a spot."

I worried my lip with my teeth.

"You working?"

He shrugged. "Yeah."

I wasn't actually sure what Ghost did.

At first, I'd thought he was a law enforcement officer. But he was a little too free at handing out punishments, and any time a LEO walked in the door, Ghost walked out the back.

He helped them, yes, but he didn't actually work with them.

He did his own private work, and it was rarely ever that I saw him doing his job…at least I didn't think I did, anyway.

Though, I had never been to his house. He worked from home the majority of the time, and since he never allowed anyone to come to his place, none of us could ever confirm what it was he did.

So, him actually saying he was working instead of beating around the subject was enough to set off some red flags.

"Well, let's go," I said. "See you later, Dad."

My father frowned at me, at Ghost, and then in the direction I assumed Naomi was still sitting.

"We riding?" I asked as I walked out the back door. "Or do you want to take my truck."

If Ghost smiled, he would've done it right then.

"Ride."

"What's up?" I asked as I walked toward my bike. "Something wrong?"

"Thought you needed an excuse to get out of there. And I need an excuse not to fuck something up that's been in the works for four years now. I need to go, I just need to make sure that I don't let the crazy out when I get there."

I looked at my friend, then nodded once.

"I'm there if you need me."

He took a deep breath then released it. "I need you."

For Ghost to say something like that, I knew he really did need me.

I looked back one last time at Naomi standing in the doorway of my father's house, and knew that there was always one constant in my life...and that was my club. These men had always been there for me, even the jackwad, Jessie James, a time or two.

Without another thought, I turned my back on Naomi, and walked down the driveway to my bike.

***

"You need to give her a break, Son," my father said. "She was scared, in a town where she didn't know anyone, and honestly, she doesn't even owe you an explanation. She owes you less than nothing. You gave her an orgasm, that was it."

I refrained from saying 'and how do you know that?' But just barely.

"I don't remember asking for your opinion," I observed, staring up at my old man.

I picked up the bottle of water I'd filled from the fridge, and turned, not bothering to wait for the man's rebuttal. I knew he had one.

I also knew that he liked Naomi.

Hell, I did, too. Which was the problem.

She'd fucking left me in my bed, gone to work, and then had disappeared. Without a single word.

I didn't know if she was hurt. Didn't know if she was okay. Didn't know if I should be assembling a posse to start looking for her. I didn't know a goddamned thing.

I'd gone by her house to find it empty. Then had called into work to see if they'd heard anything from her before she left, only to be informed that I'd have a new partner for a few weeks while Naomi took care of some personal issues.

I had no clue if those personal issues had anything to do with me since the woman hadn't even bothered to answer her goddamned phone.

I'd spent the next few days in a state of constant worry until yesterday evening when a nurse from the hospital called to inform me that my 'friend Naomi' was there and that she'd asked me to pick her up tomorrow when she was discharged.

I'd jumped at the chance, but after days of stewing in anger and worry, I wasn't in a good place.

So by the time I'd gotten to the hospital to pick her up the next afternoon, I was one seriously pissed off man who wanted to hurt her with my words instead of telling her I'd missed her like crazy.

Apparently, we hadn't shared what I'd thought we'd shared, and it'd all been in my imagination, just like always.

Which led me to now, two days later, taking Naomi to the fucking walking trail again so she could share two hours with her new friend instead of talking to me.

"Ready?" I barked, startling Naomi who was just coming out of her room.

She bit her lip, then nodded once.

"Yes."

She said that so quietly that I crossed my arms across my chest to keep myself from reaching for her.

"Then get in the truck."

At least she was well enough now to get in by herself.

If I had to put my hands on her, I wasn't going to be responsible for what I did.

For what I wanted to do.

Apparently, being mad at the woman didn't take away from the fact that I wanted her.

No, life was a cruel bitch like that.

***

Naomi

"The man, though he hasn't professed his love, really cares about you. I could tell that the day he picked you up from the hospital."

I bit my lip and looked away from the greasy guy who'd finally managed to pass us, letting my eyes take in the grass that was lining the trail we were currently walking at a crawl-like pace on.

I'd been seeing that same greasy guy everywhere I went over the last few days.

"I don't know about that," I said to Brady. "He doesn't act like he likes me all that much."

"That's because you upset him. He doesn't know how to deal with the fact that his girl would have major surgery without telling him. Instead of taking his feelings into consideration, you dismissed them in an attempt to protect yourself from potentially being disappointed. You left him the day before in a good place, and the next day you totally disregarded anything he might have been feeling. How do you expect him to react?"

That was so true.

I would react much the same way, and I only had myself to blame.

I frowned down at my feet.

"When my Molly and I married, she never kept a single thing from me. Until the day she found out she had cancer."

That dropped between us like a two-ton elephant, and I had no clue what to say.

"She took that from me. Those hours that I would've sat by her side, she stole, thinking she was saving me from heartache." He sounded lost. "Had I known that she was getting treatment, I would've been at her side, holding her hand. By not telling me, she robbed me of that and that time we could have spent together. I would've done anything for her, but now she's gone, and I don't know who I am anymore."

Tears started to trickle down my cheeks.

"I'm furious. I want to yell and scream and curse. But I can't." He looked down at me. "You wanna know why?"

I knew why.

Because she was gone.

"I see you have your answer."

I did.

"Why are you crying?"

I looked up to find Sean standing there, waiting for me.

He'd dropped me off at the trail, just like he'd done the day before, and he ran in the opposite direction while we walked the short route.

Then he waited patiently for me to return before he drove me back to his dad's house and then left for the rest of the day.

He didn't always leave the premises. Most of the time he went over to his father's shop and worked on his project motorcycle either with his father or by himself.

I, on the other hand, was unsure of my welcome so I stayed where I was, bored to tears.

The one and only time I ventured out there to where he was, he'd totally ignored me.

I felt like I wasn't wanted, so I'd gone inside without saying a single word to him in ten whole minutes.

"Mr. Thorton was telling me about his marriage and his wife," I finally settled on. "It was sad."

His eyes took in my face, the tears still coursing down my cheeks, and then turned his attention to my walking companion.

"You need a ride home today?"

That question was directed at Mr. Thorton, not me. I wouldn't have a choice where I went.

I'd tried to leave.

Twice, in fact.

Both times I did, I found myself stopped before I could even get out of the driveway. Both times, Sean had dragged me back, even the second time when I'd waited until he was asleep with the lights off to try.

Though, I realized now, it was a mistake to ever think that Sean didn't have eyes in the back of his head, because he did.

It was obvious, even to me, that he had to have some eyes somewhere. Cameras, or a movement alarm.

Hell, I didn't know. I just knew and I didn't try to escape anymore. Not after being on the receiving end of his blank stare that told me without words that the next time I tried that, he'd spank my ass—fucked up bowels or not.

"No, son," Mr. Brady said. "But I'd love for you to put Butterfinger in my car. It hurts me to lift her sometimes."

I looked down at Butterfinger.

She was an overweight Rottweiler who clearly needed to go on a diet…yesterday.

"Sure," Sean said with so little enthusiasm I nearly laughed. "Can you unlock your truck?"

Mr. Thorton drove a small, thirty-year-old Nissan truck that clearly had been well taken care of. What hadn't been taken care of, though, were the tires.

Tires that even I knew that he needed. A woman who had no clue when it came to anything car-related.

Hell, the only time I knew something was wrong with my car was when the beeping or warning lights started to appear.

Mr. Thorton handed Butterfinger's leash over to Sean.

The moment Sean had the leash, Butterfinger dropped to her haunches and glared up at Sean.

"I don't understand what I did," he sighed. "I've never had a dog *not* like me."

I wanted to say something along the lines of, 'Maybe he's reading that you hate me right now' but chose not to open the can of worms.

It wouldn't be good to deal with this now, in public with the whole freakin' morning rush of men and women watching us hash this shit out.

I really, really tried not to laugh at what happened next.

But I couldn't help it.

The moment that Butterfinger allowed herself to be hauled across the slick concrete, half of her body in Sean's large arms and the other half stubbornly dragging behind her, I just couldn't help it.

Sean glared at me to silence my laughter, but I could only turn and watch out of the corner of my eye while I said my goodbyes to Mr. Thorton.

"You really shouldn't laugh, dear," he informed me. "And I shouldn't, either. He found my dog for me. I think that's why she hates him, though."

I agreed.

Two days earlier, Sean had disappeared for nearly the entire day, and only later that night would I get a thank you call from Mr. Thorton for having my boyfriend look for his dog.

A dog which happened to be staying at one of his neighbor's houses being fed dutifully by three kids in their parents' backyard, the parents none the wiser.

"You think it's because he's not getting fed his Twinkies and Little Debbies for dinner anymore that he dislikes Sean so immensely?" I asked for confirmation.

He nodded, smiling when Sean finally got to the truck and lifted the hundred and fifteen-pound dog into the passenger seat.

I walked forward and gave Mr. Thorton a hug.

"Be careful going home. I'll see you tomorrow, okay?"

Mr. Thorton smiled. "Yeah, but I usually don't walk on Fridays. If I walk tomorrow, I will not be walking on Saturday, okay?"

I pursed my lips, then gave the old man a kiss on the cheek.

"Yeah," I agreed. "But I'll still be here, even if you aren't."

I had to hide the smile that threatened my lips when Mr. Thorton turned on his patented glare.

"That, young lady, better not be a guilt trip."

I shrugged, then wiped my eyes with my sleeves.

"I'm not sure what you're talking about."

He rolled his eyes and walked slowly to his car.

I followed suit, but went one car past Mr. Thorton's to Sean's big blue behemoth.

I did manage to get in myself this time, though, so I was getting better. Even if it wasn't coming as fast as I would like.

"You ready?"

I turned to study the man who'd waited until I was all the way in before getting in himself.

"Yeah," I said softly, wishing I would get more than two words from him at a time. "Ready."

He started the truck up, and he drove home.

Without, I might add, saying a damn word.

Lani Lynn Vale

CHAPTER 12

If you like to spoon, you'll love to spatula. That's where I flip you over and make sure you're done properly on both sides.
-Pickup lines that don't work unless you have a beard

Naomi

Three weeks later

I was officially over Sean's shit.

As I walked out of the station and saw him up close and personal with his ex, I decided that it was high time that I either shit or got off the pot.

It'd been three weeks of nothing but Sean ignoring me, and I was officially over it.

Something needed to give, and it wasn't me.

It was him.

He either needed to forgive me, or I needed to move on, because I was tired of feeling this way.

I walked to my car, a car that I was lucky to have since Sean had been taking me everywhere for the last three weeks.

But he'd wanted to go vote on the way to work, and I'd needed to stop to get some ladies' utensils, aka tampons.

Something that he'd allowed me to do either because he didn't like dealing with women's shit, or he was tired of being around me.

Regardless, I now had my car in my possession, and things were about to get real.

The moment I got to my car, I bleeped the locks and opened the passenger side door, easily extracting a spiral bound notebook from the floorboard and started writing my note with a pen I'd found on the ground outside of a gas station the day before.

My phone vibrated in my pocket, and I bit my lip, wondering if I should answer it or write the note.

I answered the phone.

"When are you coming home?"

My mom.

"Today."

Her inhale was swift and sharp, and I smiled.

Then I wrote my note.

I don't want you to be mad at me anymore. I was being stupid. I'm a girl, and we do stupid things sometimes. But ever since I've gotten out of the hospital, you've broken my heart a little more each day. It hurts. I miss my friend. Don't be mad at me.

I placed the note on the seat of Sean's bike, hoping that it didn't blow off with a gust of wind.

With one last glance at Sean where he was talking with Ellen, I got into my car and didn't look back.

Wouldn't ever look back.

Putting my phone to my ear, I dialed my best friend and unloaded.

"I'm coming home."

***

I drove ten over the speed limit the entire way and didn't once get pulled over.

Either it was divine intervention happening, or I was just not speeding as much as other drivers.

Regardless, I pulled up in front of Aspen's house seven hours later and turned my car off in her driveway.

I didn't even make it out of my car all the way before my best friend was on me, tackling me to the ground and wrapping her legs and arms around me like a monkey on crack.

"Jesus," the breath left my lungs, whooshing out so fast that I got light headed.

"Your phone's ringing."

That was from Aspen's husband.

I looked up and grinned at Drew.

"Yeah," I acknowledged. "Been doing that for a couple of hours now."

Or six.

He allowed me an hour before he'd started calling, trying to figure out where I was.

I hadn't answered at all. The only clue he had that I left the city was that I'd at least called Big Papa and told him that I wasn't going to be home tonight.

Though, that was out of courtesy to the man I was staying with since Big Papa was a worry wart.

"I missed you so much," Aspen said, squeezing her arms tighter around my neck.

I patted her elbow.

"Yeah," I wheezed. "But if you don't let up, I might die."

She snorted.

Did her grip around my neck let up, though?

Hell no.

"People are staring, Aspen," Drew pointed out. "And your brother just pulled up."

I looked up, the inch that Aspen's grip allowed, and waved with my fingers at her brother.

He grinned at me.

"Looking a little red there, girl."

I snorted, patted Aspen's arm again to get her to let me go, and I breathed a sigh of relief when she finally did.

We both made our way to our feet, and Aspen was on me again.

"I've missed you so much. Do you think it'd be okay to…"

"No." Drew and Downy responded at the same time.

I rolled my eyes.

"We can paint each other's nails," I informed her. "But I'm not going out drinking. The doctor strictly prohibited that."

She huffed. "That's ridiculous."

I shrugged.

"Not even wine?"

I shook my head. "Nope."

"Come inside," Drew said. "And make sure you dust yourself off. Y'all have grass in your hair and on your asses."

I started to dust the grass off of my shirt, and followed Drew inside, waving at Drew's daughter who was on the phone talking to someone

She waved back but didn't disrupt her phone conversation.

"Who's she talking to?" I asked as soon as the door closed.

"Her man. He calls at the same time every day…if he can. They're doing really good together," Drew answered.

Drew's daughter had met a boy who'd gone into the military, and he'd gone on his first deployment only three months ago.

"Is she still living at the dorm in the family housing?" I asked.

Drew grunted.

I grinned.

"What's for dinner?"

My phone rang again, and I looked at Drew accusingly.

He handed it to me, and I silenced it by pressing the 'ignore call' button on the screen.

Then I shoved the thing into my pocket and crossed my arms over my chest.

"You're a stubborn bitch, you know that?"

I looked at Aspen.

"Look who's talking, felony girl."

Aspen flipped me off.

"My life isn't under scrutiny here, yours is."

I shrugged.

"Well, my life is just that—mine, and you need to butt out of it."

Aspen rolled her eyes as Downy started to chuckle.

"Do you remember that time my sister went all Carrie Underwood on your brother's cop car, and you didn't see your way out of it?" Downy butted in.

I turned my glare to him.

"This is an A and B conversation. C your way out of it."

He did spirit fingers, raising his fingers high up above his head and wiggling them. The move made him look sort of ridiculous, causing me to sigh.

"Can you at least give me until tomorrow to talk about it?" I asked.

Aspen's mouth twitched, and I moaned. "Oh, come on!"

And that was how I ended up pouring out my recent life story to my friends, who apparently didn't have anything better to do with their lives.

"So you just left, and you didn't wait to see if he had anything to say?" Aspen asked with incredulity. "That doesn't sound like you."

She was right. It didn't.

But I wasn't the same Naomi that I used to be, and the sooner everyone saw that, the better.

***

"Goodnight, Mom," I whispered, hugging my mother tighter than I would have normally.

She'd just spent the last two hours talking to me about my brother, and what her hopes and dreams had been for him.

I'd sat there, listening to her words, wondering if I should feel bad about what happened with my brother.

Should being the operative word.

I didn't feel bad. Not even a little bit. He'd done this to himself, and he only had himself to blame.

I'd stuck by his side, even after he'd screwed over my best friend in the whole wide world. Even after he'd almost gotten me fired from my job because he'd blamed me for something that he'd done.

But when he'd run me over, almost stealing my life and causing me serious bodily injury, I came to a decision.

One where I promised myself that I'd stop putting everyone else first and put me first instead.

It was this promise that kept me from calling Sean because I was putting *me* first. Even if it ruined *us* in the process.

"Love you, Mom. I'll see you tomorrow when you get home from work," I whispered into her hair.

My mother squeezed just a little bit tighter, then let me go.

With a pat to the cheek, she walked to her room and didn't once look back.

I watched her go, standing there in the doorway to my very empty childhood bedroom, and waited until her door closed to follow suit.

Once my door was closed, I looked at the room that'd been my happy place when I was growing up.

Now it just looked like an empty room.

None of my personalization was there anymore. No wacky pink paint with purple zebra stripes. No knick-knacks or posters from teen magazines or any of my old soccer trophies.

There wasn't anything. Not even any curtains.

My phone beeped again, and I looked at it, sitting on the blow-up mattress, and wondered if I should break down and call the man back.

He was relentless, I'd give him that.

I threw back the covers on the mattress, shucked my watch and rings, and placed them on the floor beside the bed.

My phone was the next to follow, getting plugged into the charger that I'd borrowed from my mother.

And when I was in nothing but a t-shirt and panties, I flipped off the light, then walked to the bathroom. Closing the door quietly, I washed my face, used the facilities, and lifted my shirt, staring at what was left of the last few months torment.

My belly looked good, really good. (As long as I ignored the stretch marks and flab.) The stoma was gone, and all that was left of it was a pink scar that was healing, and I'd been assured would fade in color over time.

I looked like any normal thirty-year-old woman would, or at least I thought I did.

My belly could be flatter, and my breasts could be larger.

My ass had cellulite, and my chin was well on its way to being double.

But I felt good. I was on the road to recovery, I was healthy, and for the most part, I was happy about where I was in life.

Sighing audibly, I yanked my shirt back down, washed my hands, and turned off the light to the bathroom before opening the bathroom door and heading to my bed.

The moment I felt my feet hit the mattress, I eased my body down onto my hands and knees, savoring the way relaxation I was feeling.

Moving into a modified downward dog position, I stayed like that, enjoying the stretch and wondering if the soreness I felt would ever go away.

It didn't feel like it ever would.

Literally, it felt like I was always sore.

Not in an 'oh my God I can't move' way, but in an 'I just worked out and it kicked my ass' kind of way.

Something loud banged outside, but I didn't move.

The neighbor had a large dog that he sometimes left outside if it was cool enough, and he was a loud son of a bitch. His name was Goober, and he was a two-hundred-pound Mastiff that looked mean as hell, but was really a big ol' baby.

Though, he did like to eat balls, toys, shoes, plants, and wooden fences.

After going outside when the neighbor had first started letting him outside at night and seeing him chewing on the chain link fence, I'd decided that I'd just let him be.

Once I got to sleep, I was a fairly sound sleeper, so it wouldn't bother me too much if he did happen to be outside tonight.

Stretched out as much as I could get, I dropped down on my belly, and once more reached for my phone, letting my finger swipe over the lock screen as I looked at all the missed calls and text messages from Sean.

Not one of them was mean, though.

Most of them were along the lines of 'call me please' or 'Naomi, please.'

The last one he'd sent, though, was short and sweet.

Sean (11:22 PM): *You better be safe. Night, beautiful.*

My heart warmed for the first time since I'd left him, I turned my phone to silent and let it drop to the floor. Then I reached over my shoulder and tugged the blanket over my hips and all the way up to my chin.

Once there, I closed my eyes and let my mind wander.

It was no surprise where it went.

That bearded man owned all of my thoughts, both waking and dreaming.

CHAPTER 13

I think we all want the same thing. Love. World peace. And to be fucked so hard that we can't go to work the next day.
-Naomi's secret thoughts

Naomi

I was in a dead sleep when I woke suddenly, feeling weird. Wind moving over my skin. A noise that sounded like a shoe moving over a hard surface.

I rolled onto my side, cracked my eyelids open slightly and stared at the open window in confusion.

Why was it open? I definitely didn't open it. It was far too cold out tonight for that, not to mention my mother would kill me for letting out the heat.

Oh God, I could just hear her now...

Naomi, do you pay the electric bill here? Was that a no? I'm sorry, can you speak up, I can't hear you. That sure sounded like a 'no' to me. I know you can't possibly being saying yes, since I know for certain that I've never once seen any money leave your pocket to help me pay this electric bill.

But there it was, the window that had been closed when I went to sleep stared back at me obviously flung wide open.

I sat up in bed, fear slithering down my spine, as I heard the unmistakable sound of a motorcycle starting up.

Just as suddenly, I heard the engine accelerate as it pulled away, leaving me wondering what in the hell had just happened and who had left.

My mother lived in a cul-de-sac. She had a neighbor on each side of her house, but they were both elderly, and I was pretty damn sure neither would be on a motorcycle in the middle of the night.

Mr. Worsham was an elderly man in his late nineties who could barely walk, let alone ride a motorcycle.

Mrs. Cooper was a seventy-nine-year-old widower whose son drive her everywhere, but only during daylight hours because she was scared to go out at night.

It wasn't anyone who lived on this street. Not because anybody here disliked motorcycles, but because this was such a quiet neighborhood that if one neighbor had one, the noise from it would draw the other neighbors' attention. If one of my mother's elderly neighbors had suddenly taken up riding a motorcycle, she'd have told me about it right away. That would be big news on her street!

There were woods at our backs that ran for over seventy miles, and it was owned by a farming family who ran their cows over the land in a rotation every three months. So I knew that the sound hadn't come from that direction.

Getting up, I walked to the window and looked out, shivering slightly at the cool night breeze that rolled through the window.

As I scanned the area, I wondered if the sound had just been a figment of my imagination. However, within thirty seconds of having that thought, another set of motorcycle pipes filled the night air of my neighborhood, bringing my attention to the street right outside my house.

I frowned, looking at the single headlight drawing closer as if it were a puzzle that was too complex for my still sleepy brain to figure out.

Then the man riding the motorcycle got off, shut the bike down and stood to his full height.

I realized who it was within thirty seconds.

"What are you doing here?" I asked as the man approached the window, heart pounding. "And when are you leaving?"

Sean's lips twitched as he walked up to where I was standing, placing his large hands on either side of the window pane.

His large, bulging biceps dominated my vision, and it was extremely hard to not stare.

Even in the barely lit night, the moon in early stages of waning, I could see the play of his muscles as he did nothing but stand there.

Those rough fingers gripped onto the brick as he stared at me through the darkness.

"I'm here because you're here," he answered simply. "And I'm not leaving until you do."

I frowned.

"What'd you just do?" I asked, referring to him leaving and then coming back.

He let one of his hands up from the window and traced a large, blunt finger down the line of my jaw.

"I found out where you were, no thanks to you, and rode straight here."

I crossed my arms over my chest, trying to ignore the way that single touch made me feel.

My belly clenched, and his lips twitched.

He knew what he did to me.

I narrowed my eyes.

"I don't want you here."

He moved, pushing me forward with a large hand to my chest as he maneuvered his hulking frame through the window.

I stared at him as he towered over me at his full height, no longer separated from me by the window, and wondered what he was going to do now.

"If you don't want me here, then I'll leave."

My heart started to pound at his words, and it took everything I had not to shout in denial.

I was lying to myself.

I didn't want him to leave. Not even a little bit.

But my mouth wasn't linked to my brain, and I spouted off when I was nervous.

"I don't want you here," I repeated.

His eyes locked on me, studying my face, and he grinned.

"That 'come hither' look you have going on is enough to make me call bullshit," he informed me, his hand moving up to cup my jaw.

Such a gentle touch from such a large man had my head whirling. He didn't look like he'd be capable of such tenderness.

"I don't know what look you're speaking of," I lied. "And you should really be ashamed of yourself, leaving my window open. My mother would curse you if she saw."

His eyes went to the window, which was still wide open, and he dropped his hand.

My heart started to twist as I thought he was leaving, but he did nothing more than pull the lower panes down and twist the lock above it before turning to look at me.

"I missed you. And I'm an asshole," he announced simply.

My shoulders slumped. He had given me the opening that I needed to apologize in person.

"I'm an asshole, too," I said. "I wanted you to be there, but I didn't want to come off as that needy girl that you just met. I didn't want you to feel sorry for me, either."

He sighed, then surprised me by removing his shirt.

When he started on his belt buckle, my heart started to untwist as blood started to pump through it.

Although I couldn't see him perfectly, my mind went back to the time when I could see him perfectly. His abs, his large bulging biceps. His strong jaw, and tapered waist.

Those large hands that did nothing but sweet things to my body.

And then there was his mouth.

That sweet, delicious mouth.

CHAPTER 14

Sean: Am I adopted?
Dad: Not yet. I haven't found anyone who's willing to take you.
-Text from Sean to Big Papa

Sean

I wrapped my arms around her back and pulled her in tight to my chest.

With her tiny body pressed against mine, I had the distinct impression that she was still reluctant for me to be there.

"I'm sorry."

The words weren't enough. I knew that.

I'd taken the hurt I'd felt when she'd left me in the dark for a week, and nursed it until it was unhealthy. I'd taken it out on her and repeatedly punished her for making the decision not to include me in her life.

I had no right to do that.

All I could say at this point was that I was sorry. That I wouldn't be that dumbass guy anymore.

She dropped her head until it rested on my sternum, nestled

between the hard wall of my pecs.

"I was a dumbass. I was hurt, and I overreacted. I should've just spoken with you, but instead of doing that, I punished us both when I didn't need to."

Her hand rose up, starting around my waist, and slowly moving in an upward motion along the line of my side. My ribs. My armpit, around my shoulder, then stopping just below my clavicle.

"I wanted to call you," she whispered.

My eyes closed.

"I wanted you to call me, too."

"I was afraid that by asking you to come, you'd feel obligated, and I wasn't sure we were at that point in our relationship yet."

I growled in frustration, wrapping my arms around her and holding on tight for a few long seconds.

"How about we both stop assuming what the other one is feeling or wants out of the relationship, and we just go from there?" I offered. "Start letting each other think for themselves."

Her hand slid back down my side, then in and across my belly as she moved it to trail her fingers through the line of hair that led down the center of my abdomen.

I caught her hand. It was like ice in my palm.

"Naomi," I tried to pull away, putting a little distance in between us as I spoke. "I'm in a real tight place right now," I informed her, stepping back one more step. "I'm on the edge, and I don't want to make this any more complicated. Plus, you just had surgery..."

"Four weeks ago," she supplied. "I'm not hurt. I'm not delicate. And honestly, I'm fucking horny. You've done nothing but tease me with your hot, sweaty body for weeks. You're here, I want you here, and I want you. There's nothing else to say to that."

There really wasn't.

If she was being honest, then it was time for me to be honest, too.

"I would want nothing more than to fuck you right now," I started. "But you make me lose my mind. I'm in a place that's not my own, and I'm not even sure I'm welcome here at this point since I'm sure you shared with your entire family, and all of your friends, the reason for your impromptu visit."

Her eyes shone with laughter. "You won't die."

I dropped my mouth to hers, kissed the ever loving shit out of her, and then released her lips. "I won't die?"

Her mouth kicked up at one side. "Correct. You won't die. They know, but they're not going to kill you while you sleep."

I moved until I could push her to the bed, Naomi's soft body moving compliantly with mine as we went.

The moment her calves met the bed, she fell back to her ass and waited for what I would do next.

"I'm fucking insane," I murmured to her before dropping down on the bed between her thighs. "Your friend's husband is going to kill me."

"Drew won't kill you," she promised. "He might scowl at you, but he understands."

I didn't really care if he understood at this point or not.

All I cared about was the fact that I had a hot, welcoming woman underneath me that I'd done nothing but dream about for the last twenty days.

"You got any condoms?"

"One," I grunted. "Enough for now."

She hummed in agreement, then started to buck her hips in little tiny jerks as I ran my tongue up the length of her jaw.

"Need to be quiet," I informed her as I bent low, taking her sweet lips.

The moment her mouth met mine, I started running my hands up the back of her shirt, slowly sliding it from her body, one slow inch at a time. However, since my hands were fumbling in the dark while I tried to contain the woman about to explode before I could even get inside of her, it took a lot longer than I would've desired.

"Had dreams about you and this," I told her gruffly, my fingers playing along the ridge of her spine. "About how you'd feel underneath of me again."

She bit her lip and stared up at me as I slowly let my fingers dance along the soft seam of her panties.

She sucked in her stomach, and I took the invitation for what it was.

The second my fingers met her pubic hair, she gasped. Her breathing was already ragged, as was mine.

Her hand moved, skimming over my belly, and stopping at my nipple.

As her soft finger played over the sensitive tip, my eyes closed and my hip jerked reflexively as my cock pressed into her bare, soft thigh.

She moaned into my throat, and my hand shifted deeper into her panties.

My fingers moved of their own volition once my hand was completely inside her silky underwear, seeking the heat between her thighs.

Due to the stretchiness of said panties, my movements weren't constricted in the least as my fingers delved between the lips of her sex.

I felt the sharp nip of her teeth on my chest, and I grinned, dropping my nose to the top of her head and inhaling deeply.

"Missed the smell of you," I told her. "Missed the way you felt underneath my hands. Missed the way you would laugh softly under your breath as you read your books. The way you twisted your fingers through a strand of hair and twirled it. Most of all, though, I missed talking to you."

She shivered in my arms.

The next few minutes played out like my dreams.

I finally dipped my fingers into her pussy, and the minute I did, she came apart in my arms.

She bucked, rode my hand, and cried out against my chest.

Luckily my shirt—which she'd somehow found and shoved over her mouth—muffled her scream, or we might've had the entire neighborhood knowing exactly what was going on in here.

The moment I was ready to flip her onto her hands and knees and thrust my cock into her hot, willing body, she pulled away and pushed at my chest at the same time, causing me to stumble back in surprise.

"What the fuck?" I barked in confusion.

She whirled around, pointed her finger, and hissed at me.

"Shut up."

Her hair fell over her shoulders, and smoothed it back over her shoulders.

My brows rose, but I held my hands up in surrender.

"What'd I do now?"

She narrowed those beautiful eyes at me, then whisper yelled at me.

"What did you not do?" she growled. "You ignored me. Left me with your dad while you went out and did Lord knows what."

She didn't actually say the words, but I knew what she meant.

"I didn't have any other woman since you," I informed her. "In fact, there hasn't been another woman since the day I met you at the station."

Her chin jerked like I'd surprised her with my words.

"You're lying," she accused. "There's no way a man like you would go weeks without getting some."

I crossed my arms over my chest.

"Well, I have no way to prove it to you," I informed her. "But I haven't. There hasn't been anyone but you because you're fucking under my skin!" My voice rose. "You're all I ever think about. It's like you're some fucking disease, like the goddamn clap, that won't go away!"

Her mouth dropped open. "Did you just compare me to chlamydia?"

My mouth twitched. "If the pustule fits."

She made a gagging sound, then walked forward and smacked me delicately on the chest.

Likely, she'd given it all she had, though, so I chose not to point out that it didn't hurt.

I caught her hand when she went to hit me a second time, and pulled her into me, clamping my arms tightly around her back so she couldn't leave.

"What else is bothering you?"

She frowned ferociously at me, and I was silently thankful that she was mine, even if she wasn't acting like it at the moment.

"I don't like seeing you with Ellen," she reported bluntly, surprising me that she would just come right out and say it.

I pulled her even closer.

"I was talking to her about you," I told her. "She told me to stop being stupid. I was already well on the way to pulling my head out of my ass when she said that."

She sighed, bringing up her thumb to nibble on the fingernail.

"I was probably overreacting on my end, too," she admitted. "But I was heartbroken, and sad, and probably PMSing."

"Probably PMSing?" I challenged, standing up. "How is that a probably?"

"Okay, I'm not. At least not yet. But I will be soon," she revealed, also climbing to her feet. "I can feel my cramps coming on as we speak."

I grinned.

"I already said I'm sorry," I told her soberly. "What else do you want me to say?"

She went up on her tippy toes and placed her mouth to mine.

I took control of the kiss, tangling my tongue with hers, and moaned when she sucked my tongue into her mouth.

"Fuck me," she whispered against my lips.

I flipped her around by her hips, flipped her hair off her shoulders, and bent her over the bed.

Her panties were the first thing to go.

Moments later I had my cock lined up with her entrance.

Sinking inside of her, I squeezed my eyes tightly shut and moaned.

She felt amazing.

My memory didn't do her justice.

The hot feel of her surrounding my cock. The way she felt so slick, wet and ready for me. The way her muscles clenched tight on the tip of my cock, a feeling that traveled down the length of my shaft as I slowly sank myself completely inside of her.

It was better than anything I'd ever had before.

Naomi mewled, pushing back against me to force me to participate.

I, on the other hand, had frozen the moment I was completely inside of her. The moment all of that dewy heat surrounded me, my balls had risen up, threatened to empty with less than a thought.

"Don't move," I whispered out roughly.

She moved.

Lifting one leg up on the bed, she started to force herself back on me, despite my hand on her hips stilling her movements.

"If you don't start moving," she snarled quietly, "I'm going to get myself off."

Before she could so much as move her hand toward that pretty clit of hers, I had both of them in my grip, holding them high at her back.

"Can't do that when you can't move your hands," I grunted.

Her head fell, and those beautiful blonde curls slipped even further from the band at the nape of her neck.

I couldn't resist the urge to wrap my fingers around the silky mass.

The moment my fingers entwined with her hair, she stopped trying to writhe on my dick, and became so still that I was worried I had hurt her in some way.

"Naomi," I whispered.

"Please move," she whispered, sounding on the verge of crying. "I want you to move."

I moved.

Slow, at first, to try to control the urge to release into her body within the first half a thrust.

After realizing it was futile, that I was going to go anyway, I let go.

Using my grip on her hands and her hair, I forced her to take me, over and over again. My cock hit so deep inside of her that it bumped into her cervix with each powerful slam home.

The only thing holding her head up was my grip in her hair, but I didn't worry that I was hurting her. I had no doubt whatsoever that she'd tell me if I was, so I continued with my hold, keeping her head where I wanted it.

The fingers of both hands were clenched on tightly to my fingers and wrist, holding on the best way she could.

The leg she had up on the bed was giving me the backward force that I needed to keep her in place and allowed me to push so deeply inside of her that I wanted to bury myself there and never crawl my way back out again.

Our flesh met, slapping together so hard that we definitely weren't being as quiet as we should have been.

My balls started to draw up, still slapping against her mound with each plunge forward, and suddenly it all came crashing down.

She came, clenching and unclenching around me like tiny little fists massaging the length of my cock, coaxing it to give it what it wanted.

I lost control, pounding so hard inside of her that it was mediocre at best.

But I couldn't help it. The way she made me feel, I couldn't think rationally.

Couldn't make my brain move as fast as it should be.

And then, with a sudden understanding, I realized why she felt so fucking good. Realized why it was ten times better than I remembered.

I managed to pull out, barely, shooting my seed all over the soft lips of her sex, crack of her ass, and back.

I watched as my come ran down her leg, and released her hand to catch it.

She was faster, catching it with her hand and swiping it up her leg to cup her sex.

"I don't have anything to clean up with, and I'm worried if I start moving, it'll all go everywhere. And I really, really don't want to explain to my mother why I got jizz on her carpet," she murmured worriedly. "How am I going to clean this up?"

I found myself smiling.

Backing away from her, I looked around the room for something to use.

The glow from the full moon didn't offer that much light, though, so I walked to the door and flipped on the light switch, wincing when the bright light lit up the room around us.

"You're standing in front of an open window with a light on, and the street is right there," Naomi whisper yelled.

I gave her a look that clearly said 'really?'

She bared her teeth at me.

"You're in a cul-de-sac. There are two elderly people on either side of you and a fifty something year old man that lives on the corner. He isn't home, because as I was arriving, he was leaving. He had a travel mug of coffee, which indicates he wasn't planning on coming back any time soon," I informed her.

She blinked.

"That was Mr. Monk. He's a marathon runner, and wakes up at the crack of dawn to get his ten miles in before work at nine," she uttered.

My mouth twitched.

"So no, I'm not worried about anyone seeing me. Old people can't see in the first place, and there are no lights on in their houses for me to be worried about them being up at four in the morning."

She just shook her head and started waddling awkwardly to the bathroom.

I grinned at her retreating back the entire way.

***

The next morning, I rose with the birds, after two hours of sleep, to find the house full of people.

I could hear them all talking in the living room, not trying to be quiet in the least.

That didn't bother me, though.

It was ten in the morning.

They didn't know that I'd driven to Kilgore from Alabama on less than an hour of sleep. They didn't know that I'd nearly wrecked my motorcycle yesterday on the way over here.

Though, that likely had to do with the motorcycle that had cut me off on the interstate.

I'd had the privilege of staring at his silver fucking ponytail on and off the entire way.

He'd actually taken the exit to Naomi's house, while I'd had to go to my friend Jack's place to get directions to Naomi's and shake his hand for helping me get the information on her so fast.

Slipping into my jeans from last night and the same black t-shirt that had more than a little road dust on it, I made my way out Naomi's door to find the entire population of Kilgore standing in the kitchen.

It didn't surprise me to find the cool eyed stare of Drew, Naomi's best friend's husband, directly on me the moment I came out of the room. Nor the eyes of her mother, best friend, and another man I didn't know.

The only one not looking at me was Naomi, who was busy turning bacon over on a large skillet in the corner of the kitchen.

Her friend was on one side of her, and the large man whose name I didn't know was on the other.

I nodded my head at Drew, thankful that Jack had supplied me with photos of the best friend and her husband so I'd have an idea of who everyone was before I arrived.

Now, as I stared at the fiercely protective eyes of the older man, I realized that Naomi had a true ally on her side.

"Sean," I held out my hand.

It took the other man a moment to take it, but eventually he did.

"You hurt her."

I did.

"I made her all better," I supplied.

His eyes narrowed.

"She's had enough jerking of her chain. If you're not serious, you need to leave now before she becomes attached."

I crossed my arms over my chest and stared at the man unblinkingly.

"Sean, do you want four eggs like usual?"

I looked up then, found Naomi's eyes on me, and nodded my head. "Yeah, that'd be great."

She grinned at me and turned around to grab eggs.

"Take a seat," Drew ordered.

I ignored him.

Instead, I walked up behind Naomi, squeezed in between her friend and the man, and wrapped my arms around her belly.

"Everything feel okay?" I whispered into her ear, running my hand over her belly in worry.

I'd forgotten in my haste to have her last night that she was still sore, but she hadn't once complained about my rough treatment last night. And now, with the light of day and my sanity returning, I suddenly felt awful about how I'd taken her so hard the night before.

She shivered.

"Perfect," she promised. "Have a seat and I'll bring you your food."

I placed a kiss to her forehead and retreated to the seat Drew had indicated with a tilt of his head a few moments ago.

The moment my ass hit the chair, I turned my attention to Naomi's mother.

"Sean," I held out my hand.

She grinned widely, the move so much like her daughter that it was eerie. "Masha."

"Masha," I shook the delicate hand she placed in mine. "It's nice to finally meet you. Naomi is always talking about you. She forgot to mention how much y'all look alike, though. You look like her older sister."

And she did.

She didn't look like a mother to an almost thirty-year-old.

Masha's cheeks pinked at the compliment. "I had my son when I was young. Sixteen. Naomi came two and a half years later. We don't look like mother and child, that's for sure."

My eyes widened.

Masha's eyes were lit with laughter.

"I graduated high school at seventeen, and married Danny and Naomi's father a week after that. Naomi was actually planned. He was in the military. Was killed while he was overseas."

My heart sank.

"She never got to meet her father, but she reminds me of him every time she opens her mouth." Masha's words were soft, only for me to hear.

"What branch was he in?" I asked hesitantly.

"The Army," she answered. "He was a Ranger."

I nodded.

One of the best.

"I'm sorry for your loss," I murmured. "I've lost a lot of friends during my time in the military," I told her. "It was never easy."

Her smile was soft.

"You know my daughter tells me almost everything, but you she kept close to her heart," she murmured. "I heard about you very rarely, but every time she did deign to speak of you, I could tell you were beginning to mean a lot to her."

The kitchen chair was pushed aside, and I looked up just as Naomi placed a plate with my breakfast down in front of me.

"Thanks, baby," I murmured, picking up the fork she'd placed down next to the plate.

She followed up by bringing me a cup of coffee and a glass of orange juice.

After squeezing her thigh, I dug in.

It wasn't until I was pushing my plate away that I realized I was the first one served.

"Shit," I said, looking around at the people looking at me. "Was I supposed to wait?"

Naomi's friend, Aspen, started to snicker.

"No," she remarked. "It's just not every day that Naomi doesn't feed herself first. She's selfish like that."

My brows rose. "That's not selfish. She's got that rockin' body that has to be nurtured to continue to look as delicious as it does. How else do you expect her to keep it?"

Aspen stared at me for a few long seconds, then threw her head back and laughed.

Drew touched his hand to the top of Aspen's head and took a seat on her opposite side. "You taking a seat, PD, or are you just going to stand there all day?"

PD, the man that'd voiced nothing since I'd entered the room, looked at Drew for a few long moments, and then came to take a seat on the other side of Drew.

The table that was in the middle of Masha's bright yellow kitchen, decorated in sunflowers, wasn't small, but the moment it had three very large men surrounding it, it looked tiny.

I finished off the last of my eggs, then placed my fork down on the plate and looked at the man who'd broken Naomi's heart.

"So, you're PD," I drawled. "How's the wife?"

PD's face turned from stone to humor in three seconds. "My wife just found out she's pregnant with our second child. She's currently cursing me and every man with a penis between his legs."

I snorted.

"She have morning sickness again?" Naomi asked as she started to set down plates.

"Yeah," PD said, backing away so she could place his in front of him. "Bad. Worse than last time, according to her."

The sad thing was that PD hadn't been around for the last pregnancy, so all he had to go on was what she told him.

Naomi's answering smile wasn't one of sadness, but of happiness.

And when she sat on my lap to eat her own breakfast, I realized that she was just as over PD as I was over Ellen.

We'd healed each other.

CHAPTER 15

I've reached an age where my mind says, "I can do that." But my body says, "Try it and die, fat girl."
-Fact of life

Naomi

"Why don't you like your name?" I asked the old man, two weeks after I'd visited my family in Kilgore.

He looked over at me where I was walking at his side and grinned.

I could tell, at one point, the man had been beautiful. Very handsome.

"I like my name," he said. "But I liked it more when my wife said it."

Sadness welled inside of me.

"Tell me how y'all met."

His smile was radiant.

"The Korean War."

I blinked.

"You met while fighting the Korean War?" I asked.

He smiled down at me.

"I met my Molly when I was twenty, and four days away from deployment," his words were whimsical, and I tried hard not to stare at him.

He was making my heart hurt with all his happiness on his face at remembering his wife, and how they met.

"I was going to a bar to meet my friends," he started. "One last hoorah before we all left."

I stepped over a dog who was a bit too overzealous with his excitement and waved at the frazzled looking girl trying to corral him. Butterfinger growled low in his throat but didn't make a move towards the other dog. I had started holding the dog's leash during our walks, so he could concentrate on walking.

She waved back, and I returned my eyes to Brady.

"I walked in that tavern that night, sixty some years ago, my eyes jumped to the bar area and I froze in the doorway."

"Why?" I smiled. "Was she sitting at the bar?"

He shook his head.

"No, she was dancing around it." His smile was so soft and sweet that my eyes smarted. "She had on this black dress. I'll never forget it. The skirt was big and it just spun around her knees and made her waist look so tiny. It was open at the neck and it seemed to wrap around her shoulders like it was hugging her. She looked so beautiful, I couldn't take my eyes off of her.

He swallowed. "And these bright red high heels."

I grinned.

"The high heels got you, didn't they?" I asked.

He laughed, his voice shaky.

"Yeah, they got me." He turned his eyes up to the sky, studying a giant buzzard that was circling over the path on long, languid sweeps of his wings. "And that smile. God, it made my chest tight to see that smile aimed in my direction."

We finally rounded the last path, and I saw my man. The one who I only recently discovered was mine.

And his back was stiff, his hands clenched at his sides.

Brady kept talking, unaware of what we were walking into.

"I spent every waking minute with my Molly for the next three days, and on the day that I deployed, she waved at me until the bus disappeared." He cleared his throat. "I came home a different man, but she helped put my broken mind back together again. We married two years after we met and had five kids together. Four of whom are now gone. One is in a nursing home not far from mine."

I looked away from Sean. "Kind of young to be in a nursing home."

He nodded, eyes solemn.

"Heart disease runs in our family. On my Molly's side," he murmured regretfully. "All of my children suffered heart attacks. Donnie, my youngest, is the only one to survive his."

Brady's life kept getting sadder and sadder.

Jesus, I felt like shit for even bringing up how he'd met his wife.

"I...*what in the world?*"

I looked where he was staring, and I felt my heart get tight.

Someone was burning a flag!

And oh, God! Sean was standing there, about to lose it.

"Oh shit," I said, hurrying forward.

Brady shuffled as fast as his cane and bad leg would allow him behind me, but I didn't wait.

Instead, I ran up to Sean's side, latching onto his straining arm.

It was clear to me that he was only seconds away from blowing up, and this needed to de-escalate quickly or someone—likely Sean—would make cause chaos to ensue.

"Sean," I whispered frantically. "Come with me."

He didn't budge when I tried to pull him, and I had a sinking sensation fill the pit of my belly. I knew he was closer to that line than I realized.

"Sean," I repeated.

His eyes, however, were focused on the group of what appeared to be college students and church protestors burning up a flag.

They held signs that read, 'Too late to pray' and 'You deserve those tears.'

And I realized then that this was a 'peaceful protest' of a veteran's funeral, possibly even the zealot group from Westboro Baptist Church.

There were about fifty of them, all surrounding the path of the walking trail, and trickling out into traffic.

I wasn't sure if the protest had started at the mouth of the trail so they could walk down it, or if they'd just ended up at the start of the trail because they were stopping traffic on one of the busiest streets in Mooresville.

Regardless of what they'd intended, they were now not only disrupting the traffic on the road, but also causing a whole lot of ruckus in the area and offending every single citizen, not just the Veterans, in the general vicinity.

"The funeral procession is supposed to take this route in about five minutes," I heard one of the protesters say. "Get your flags ready."

A kid stood up, and reached for another flag that he had left carelessly laying on the ground.

The minute it was in his hand, he reached for the lighter that another boy was holding out to him and struck the ignitor with his thumb to spark the lighter when Brady, cane in one hand and holding onto a park bench with the other, brought down the cane on the boy whose intention was to burn the flag.

Right over the back of the other kid's head.

The boy was stunned, falling to his knees, and dropping the lighter before it could so much as flame.

Sean jerked as he seemed to get his wits about him and finally moved.

Butterfinger, who was still in my hold at my side, lurched forward, trying to get to her master, and would've taken me down to my knees had Sean not waded in.

Grabbing Butterfinger before she could even make it a step, he pulled her over to the dog park and locked her behind the fence before turning back to the crowd that was now circling Brady.

Brady, who looked not one single bit concerned about the angry mob that was surrounding him, started yelling at the kids.

"This is my flag!" he bellowed. "I fought for this flag! I bled for this flag! I lost friends and family for this flag. All so you all could do dumb shit like this instead of using the brains that God gave you!"

Oh. *Shit.*

The crowd moved in even closer, surrounding Brady.

But then Sean was there, parting the crowd with his bare hands and a whole lot of strength.

"Move!"

Sean's bellow made everyone in the vicinity freeze, and slowly part until Brady was able to extricate himself from the sea of protesters.

"You will not burn another flag," Sean's words were horrific in their power and anger. "Or I will make sure your hands don't work to light another fucking lighter."

Those simple, short, bold words were said out of lips that I adored.

"You can try to make us."

Sean's eyes turned to a smartass girl standing on the edge of the crowd. He was so calm, that I wondered if the other shoe was going to drop.

"Let me see. Delaney, right?"

The girl looked startled.

"Isn't your brother in the Marines?"

Delaney looked startled that Sean would know that.

"N-no."

Sean smiled; it wasn't a pretty smile, either.

In fact, it was quite intimidating.

Which was felt by some of the other protesters because they all took a few steps back and looked around nervously. There had to be at least fifty of them, and every single one of them was watching Sean like he was a freakin' army instead of a single man.

"I was there when he came home from his last deployment. Part of his welcome home party, actually. I know who your brother is, and I know who you are." He frowned at the girl. "Though, I thought your parents raised you better than this."

Sean's head turned. "And you."

He pointed at the boy who had passed her the lighter.

"Isn't your mother retired from the Army?"

And so it went.

I was so surprised by the number of people Sean knew that I wasn't paying attention to the kid on the ground who Brady had struck until he was up on his knees. He was swinging a stick that he'd found right at my man who didn't notice until it was too late.

The stick hit Sean in the back of the thigh, missing his knee by only a few scant inches.

The stick broke over the back of Sean's leg, and the reaction it drew from Sean was that he staggered forward slightly, trying to avoid stepping further into the crowd of protesters any more than he already was.

The crowd went silent, and I started toward Sean to make sure that he was all right, but Brady grabbed my arm before I could even make it a step.

"Sean!" I cried out.

Sean looked down at the kid, then reached forward and picked him up by the collar of his shirt.

And by up, I mean the kid was dangling above the ground, the tips of his sneaker covered toes just barely grazing it.

"I served my country for years," he announced to the stupid kid. "I watched two of my best friends in the whole world die after by rifle fire during an attack on our unit. Held their hands while blood pumped out of their chests, as they cried and asked me to tell their wives and kids that they loved them. To tell their mothers that they were sorry. Tell their fathers that they would miss throwing the ball around on Christmas."

My throat constricted.

"I watched a female soldier being cut down from a tree where she hung herself because she couldn't live with the aftermath of killing women and children who were committing acts of war against us. Watched the medics clean up pieces of her head from where she used a gun to commit suicide because she couldn't deal with the ghosts in her head or the way she always felt fucking dirty," he continued to growl. "My father fought for that flag. My grandfather, too. And his father before him. So, let me tell you something, you little entitled son of a bitch, this country doesn't owe you a *goddamn thing* except fucking jail time. It should be a felony to burn this flag, but I fought for your fucking rights, so of course, you'll never see it. But that doesn't mean that you don't deserve it."

With that, Sean threw the kid to the ground, and the crowd sucked in a swift inhalation of breath as Sean turned, pointed at them all in turn, and gave them his back as he walked toward us.

Brady had a smile on his face the size of which I'd never seen before, and pride was practically bursting from my chest at seeing my man's show of strength and pride in his country.

"You're so hot," I told him.

Sean's face cracked into a small smile. One that was gone almost before it was even there. One that didn't reach his eyes.

But it was a start and that was all that mattered.

"Good man," Brady said to Sean.

Sean's answering reply was harsh, but nonetheless true.

"I'm fucking sick of this. This country is raising a bunch of pussies, and it keeps getting worse and worse."

I agreed, but the only thing I could change was how I raised my own kids to deal with whatever was happening with this country.

"You'll have to start with your own kids," I told him honestly. "Because you can't start with any that aren't yours. They've already been ruined by their parents' beliefs and bad upbringing."

I gestured to the kids that were still holding their signs, and he sighed.

"My kids ever acted like that, I'd beat the shit out of them," he murmured. "I'd pull them away by their ears, run over all their electronics with a lawn mower like I saw some guy do to his kid on YouTube, and then force them to watch me burn it. Then I'd put the fire out by pissing on it."

I snorted.

"Duly noted."

"I was going to try to watch the funeral procession from here, but I can't see a damn thing," Brady grumbled. "Do you think they'll move and allow me to leave? If I can get out, I can park at the top of my street and watch from there."

Sean grunted. "I'll make sure of it."

And he did.

Five minutes later, he was pushing the crowd back with only a glare, and Brady waved. "See you tomorrow, Naomi."

I waved and watched until his taillights disappeared around a bend in the road, and then turned toward Sean.

"Ready to go?"

His eyes went to the protesters and then to the remains of the burned flag.

Taking two long steps toward it, he snatched up the flag from the ground where it lay like a piece of trash instead of this nation's symbol, and then gestured to the bike.

"Get on. Let's go."

I got on, and we went.

I was putting my helmet on as he pulled past them, and not one of the protesters made eye contact with either of us.

And the whole time I hugged Sean tight.

I was proud of him.

He could've allowed that situation to get out of hand instead of using his head.

But he didn't.

"Why are they being so calm now?" I yelled over the motor. "That easily could have gone the other way."

He stopped at the stop light just past the protesters and turned his head so I could hear him.

Sean shrugged. "Most protesters are generally non-confrontational. Likely, there was only one loser who wanted to burn that flag, and he did. The others didn't participate in it, but they either condoned it by not stopping him or were too stunned by him doing it to do anything about it."

That made sense. I, on the other hand, would like to think that the country I was currently living in wasn't made up of a bunch of spineless people who wouldn't take a stand against something that they knew was wrong.

Sean's hand clamped onto my wrist, and then the light turned green.

His hand lifted, and he waved at a biker who looked vaguely familiar across traffic, yet I couldn't quite place him.

Though, he did that to every motorcycle that passed, so it wasn't an indication that he actually knew the other man.

I swiveled my head so I could watch as the biker turned behind us.

He was wearing a leather jacket, black jeans, and black boots. His shirt, however, was blue. Though, it appeared black in some places due to what I assumed were grease stains.

I'd seen the man before. Actually, I'd seen him a lot.

That long silver hair of his was pretty distinctive.

I squeezed Sean tighter, and his large hand covered mine for a half an instant before he returned it to the handlebars.

I lifted my head to rest on his shoulder, allowing my helmet to lean against his head, and stared ahead of us.

The biker passed us, but I kept my head forward, staring straight ahead, and didn't allow myself to turn and study the man.

I didn't want to see him staring, because that would only give me an even greater sense of foreboding than I already had.

Almost as fast as he'd passed us, he started slowing down.

I saw Brady, out of his car, eyes on the road behind him rather than on us, but I waved at his back anyway.

The biker that Sean waved to turned down the road that Brady was parked on, and my brows furrowed in contemplation.

Maybe that was why I saw him so much, because he lived on Brady's street.

As we rode further away, I realized that I'd been making a bigger deal of it than I should have. If the man lived on Brady's street, then I'd have seen him a lot. Brady and I had gotten thick as thieves since we'd met.

Something in my gut loosened at the knowledge that I wasn't being followed by some random scary, greasy biker dude. And I started to enjoy my ride.

Though, even when my mind was racing about some fake stalker that I'd made up, I'd been pasted up against a sexy man's back, so it hadn't been *that* bad.

Sean took the long way home, looping around the entire town on back roads, allowing me the time to breathe easy.

Rides on the back of Sean's bike were the best.

Rides where Sean wasn't wearing his cut—which allowed me to feel his spectacular muscles and nothing else but a sweaty t-shirt in between us—were even better.

Not that I had a problem with Sean wearing his club colors.

In fact, any other time I adored when he wore it. I love the way it looked on him, and how he acted when he was wearing it—like something was different about him. More confidence. More pride. More carefree.

Whatever it was, the man looked sexy in his Dixie Wardens cut.

It was only when I had my face pressed against it that I didn't adore it as much, but I was slowly getting used to it.

Sean took a turn, and I looked around, trying to figure out where we were.

"What is this?" I asked ten minutes later as he brought the bike to a stop under a tall pine tree that was bigger around than I was.

"This," he put forth, kicking the bike stand down and standing up. "Is mine."

My head tilted.

"Yours?"

He nodded.

"My land."

Understanding dawned. "When did you get this?"

He offered me his hand and I took it, dismounting the bike and falling into his side all in one jerk of his hand.

"I got this last year, but I haven't had much time to stop and see it. Barely have time to pay for it."

That, I understood too well.

The man worked a lot. Had started working even before the vacation that he was able to finagle out of our employer was up.

Even now that we were both back at work, he still worked a lot.

I worked a lot, too, but that was only because if I didn't then I'd never see him.

I'd asked him why he did it, but I didn't know that he had to do it to pay for land that I didn't even know he had.

"Why don't you park your trailer here?" I asked, looking up at him. "Then you'd get to see it a lot."

His mouth firmed.

"I bought it to build a house on with Ellen."

My belly rolled, and I started to pull away.

He stopped me by clamping his hand around my hip, refusing to allow me to move.

"At the time, our relationship was already deteriorating. I knew she had a thing for Jessie. Saw it with every breath I took. I bought this place—which was twice my budget—in the hopes that she'd love it. But she didn't."

Why that made me irrationally happy, I didn't know. But it did. I wanted to jump up and clap that she was too stupid to see that she had such a good thing and had let it go.

Had she not done that, I wouldn't be standing here, in Sean's arms, on some land meant for her.

"That was the day that she told me that she didn't do 'country' living. She didn't like bugs. She liked paved streets and being close to the city so she could go shopping." He dropped his mouth to my head, and my tense body tensed even further. "I realized something while you were gone."

I froze.

"I'd already started planning our life out here. Thinking about what you would like and not like when it came to a house. Wondered if I could convince you to move in with me when we'd only known each other for a few months."

I turned my head up so I could see if he was sincere.

His eyes were on the gate that was blocking our access to the rest of the land.

Then he tugged me forward and we were walking.

Up a long winding red clay driveway that likely would be a bitch if it rained. Through it was lined with trees that were high and beautiful beyond belief. Then that long driveway turned into a sprawling meadow, and I knew that this was where the house would go.

"Right here," I told him.

He stopped, and we looked at the land before us.

"I want to put a house there, on the top of the hill."

He echoed my thoughts exactly.

"I want to leave as many of the trees as we can and to disrupt the look of the land as little as possible," he explained. "I want a shop where I can work on my bikes and cars. I want a…"

"Pond would look good right here," I pointed to a really low lying spot where the land dipped sharply into what looked like a creek at the very bottom.

"There's a year-round creek right there," he informed me, confirming my suspicions. "And I've thought about damming it up right there and doing the same."

I grinned and pulled away from him, walking down the steep hill to the creek beyond.

CHAPTER 16

You're allowed to like other people. You just have to like me more.

-Text from Sean to Naomi

Sean

I watched as Naomi walked down the deep ravine that led to the creek below, her hand down at her side to catch herself if she started to lose her footing, and wondered how I got this lucky.

Naomi was my saving grace. The one woman who'd changed my life and made it into everything I'd ever wanted.

I'd been putting off bringing her here.

I didn't want to know if she hated it. Didn't want to see the same look on her face that I'd seen on Ellen's.

But today, after all that bullshit with the burning flags, I realized that I needed to stop being a little bitch and make my move.

I needed to either bring her into my world, or get rid of her, because I was falling fast. I was falling hard. And I didn't care. I liked where I was about to land.

My eyes strained down to her ass, which filled out those yoga pants spectacularly.

Looking at that view everyday wouldn't hurt, either.

"Are you coming or what?"

My eyes traveled from her ass to her face, and I grinned.

Shoving my hands into my pockets, I started down the steep hill, catching up to her easily with my long strides.

She huffed at me as I caught up to her and then passed her, and I turned around to laugh at her only to catch her jumping at me.

I caught her, easily, and glared at her.

"You shouldn't be doing that," I chastised her.

"Yes, Dad," she drawled sarcastically.

I moved my hands around to come to a rest under her butt, and squeezed it lightly.

"Ouch," she snapped her hips forward. "That hurt."

I turned my face, waited, and was rewarded when she placed her lips to mine.

I took a step down onto a rock that led to the creek, and came to a stop, waiting for her to get down.

She didn't.

"You getting down?"

She shook her head, shrugged, and wrapped her legs tighter around me. Her arms followed suit, choking off my airway, and her chin came to a rest on my shoulder, her face pressed against mine.

"You have food in your beard," she pointed out after a while.

I shook my head.

"I can either reach up, letting you go in the process, and remove it. Or you can do it for me, and stay where you are," I muttered darkly.

She snickered.

"Not funny," I said. "You ate breakfast with me. How could you not see that I had food in my beard?"

Her giggling was making it really hard to hold onto my scowl.

"I didn't see it until I was right here," she admitted, reaching forward and plucking something out of my beard.

She held it out to me to see, and I shook my head.

"Hot sauce," I said. "Throw it down."

She pressed her mouth into my neck, and started to snicker once again. "I thought you were saving it for later."

I pinched her ass, causing her to squirm in my hold.

"If you look over there, that's the neighboring property," I jerked my chin in the direction I wanted her to look.

She did, and frowned. "That's kind of close. What if they build a house or something right there? Then they'll be able to see into your oasis."

Hearing her obvious pleasure as she discussed the land made my heart happy.

"I didn't want you to think that you were a substitute," I told her bluntly. "That's why it took me so long to show you. Plus, I wanted to make sure that what we have between us is real."

She squeezed my neck tighter, cutting off circulation to my head.

"Can't breathe," I squeaked out.

She let up, but not before placing a kiss on my quickly reddening forehead first.

Then she patted me on the shoulder and started to squirm.

Understanding she wanted down, I dropped her legs, and she did the rest of the work.

"What's down here?" she asked, pointing in the direction of a wooded area that I hadn't gotten a chance to explore yet.

"I don't know," I admitted. "We have another hour or so before we need to head home and catch a nap before work. If you want, we can walk that way. When we get tired, we'll turn around."

She looked skeptically at the sheer drop that led even further down into the woods.

"I'm going to bust my ass, possibly break my arm, and have to skip work because I'll be in the ER getting a cast fitted onto my arm. As long as you're okay working with someone you don't like, I'll do it."

I gave her a look that clearly relayed what I thought about her trust in me and held out my hand.

She didn't even hesitate.

Placing her hand into mine, I helped her down the hill.

And not once did she fall.

Me, on the other hand…yeah, I was a different story.

***

"Oh, my God," Naomi's eyes were bright. "Are you sure you're okay?"

I looked over at her for the fifth time in less than an hour.

I was driving the medic, and trying hard not to laugh at the horror that was still pasted on Naomi's face.

"I'm fine," I promised her for the final time. "Drop it, okay?"

She bit her lip, but her eyes stayed on my eyebrow where I was now the proud new owner of fifteen stitches.

It started at the bridge of my nose and curled around my eye, stopping just above my eye socket on my left side. I had no eyebrow, though you couldn't tell really since the stitches were now acting as a temporary one.

"Does it hurt?" she whispered.

I shook my head.

"No."

I was lying. It hurt like a motherfucker.

I didn't want her to feel worse than she already did, though, so I kept silent on how much it was throbbing.

Since I couldn't take any pain meds while I was at work, I was stuck with feeling the sharp ache despite taking both Tylenol and Motrin.

"It looks like it hur…"

"Naomi, I'll smack your ass if you ask that again," I growled.

I'd fallen.

Oh, boy had I fallen.

And not gracefully, either.

I'd just helped Naomi over a fallen log, and had put my weight on it to hop over myself.

The weight of my body had been a lot more than Naomi's, and seconds after my full body weight had been on it, it collapsed out from under me.

I fell, face forward, straight into a stump and split my eye open.

"You could've lost your eye," she continued.

I sighed.

"I really, really don't want to talk about this right now," I grumbled. "So, if you'd please shut up, I'd appreciate it."

She started to snicker, and I narrowed my eyes at her.

"I'm not eating Taco Bell again," she declared once she'd managed to compose herself. "I haven't tried it since I got my colostomy reversal, but I just don't think my belly can handle it."

I hummed in approval. "I think that's acceptable. So you either have Subway, which happens to be on the way home. Or Fanny's."

Fanny's wasn't really on the way home, but I could make it on the way home. They'd never notice if I stopped in and grabbed the food.

"Fanny's," she said excitedly. "I've never had it, but I've heard that it's good."

It was. "The best," I promised. "Call ahead. Tell them you want two specials."

"What's the special?" she asked as she took her phone out of her pocket and started googling the number.

She'd just gotten on the line with them when the tones dropped.

"Medic 33, child sick and lethargic at 777 Pointy Grove Lane."

My stomach dropped.

"Oh, God," Naomi echoed my thoughts. "Never mind."

Naomi hung up the phone and I swung around a slow driving car, flipping on my lights at the same time.

The drive to the house was silent and tense, and by the time we arrived, the sick feeling in my stomach had turned to a deep ache that resonated in my bones.

It took three minutes and thirty-seven seconds to respond to the call.

This was going to be very bad. I knew it before I'd even gotten out of the medic.

"Shit," Naomi said, seeing the parents standing in the street. "I'll grab the doors."

I didn't wait to see if she got them or not. The minute I had the ambulance in park, I was running toward the front of the house as fast as my legs would take me.

My head no longer hurt, and my eyes were focused on my target.

The little baby in her mother's hysterical arms.

I'll remember the sight for the rest of my life.

The little girl was nearly naked, the only thing covering her tiny body was a white diaper with a little yellow stripe up the middle.

One tiny leg and one tiny arm were flopping loosely in the near freezing night air. Likely when she'd been holding her, the blanket had been swaddling her little body. Now the hot pink blanket only accentuated how very pale the baby was.

The minute I was in reaching distance, I took the limp child from her mother's arms and ran to the ambulance.

It took me less than twenty seconds.

I placed the little girl down on the backboard, listened to the doors slam behind me, and started CPR.

***

I dropped down to my knees after leaving the ER's trauma bay, put my hands behind me head, and hunched my body in on itself.

I couldn't find any breath in my lungs. They were burning, right along with my eyes.

Tears threatened, and the only thing that was holding them back was the fact that I had an audience.

Had I been alone, they'd be flowing freely down my cheeks to disappear into my beard.

Even now, I wasn't sure whether I could make it back to the medic without breaking down.

Hell, I was in the middle of the damn ambulance entrance to the ER, and I couldn't find it in me to move.

"Sean," Naomi whispered. "Look at me, baby."

It took me a minute, but I finally managed to look up at her.

The harsh brightness from the lights lighting the ambulance bay hurt my eyes, but I looked anyway.

"She's going to make it," Naomi promised me again.

I swallowed, nodded, and then cleared my throat.

"Yeah," I licked my lips.

She was, or at least she had a very good chance.

It'd been two minutes into CPR that she started breathing.

That tiny little body had looked so very delicate laying on that adult sized backboard.

And the needles I had in the medic weren't small enough, so I hadn't been able to start in IV.

The baby was a week or two, at most, and had been born at a mere four pounds in the first place. Her parents guestimated her weight to be around five pounds due to a doctor appointment they'd had earlier in the week. The girl likely had never even been out of her parents' loving arms.

"The parents get here yet?" I asked roughly.

She nodded, pointing to a car that was packed haphazardly in the ER drop off.

"Just got here when you came out the side door."

I nodded my head almost automatically.

"Let's go."

I got up, ignoring the sympathetic glances from my colleagues, and got into the passenger seat.

Naomi, not even questioning this, got into the driver's seat, adjusted the settings, and put it into drive.

We arrived at the station five minutes later, and I was out and moving toward the door before she'd even put it into park.

I didn't bother to think she'd leave me be, though, which was why I left my bedroom door open before I took a seat on the bed and dropped my head into my hands.

My eye throbbed, but I didn't care.

I needed the pain. Needed the proof that I was going to continue to live.

"Was that your first baby?" she asked.

I shook my head.

"No," I muttered. "Fourth."

I remembered each and every time I had a call on an infant. Three of them hadn't made it. Two of them had died from SIDS, and one of them was an accidental drowning in the bathtub when her mother left her to check on the dinner that was cooking.

This little girl was lucky to be alive, and I was grateful that I didn't have to experience the loss of an infant patient for a fourth time.

"That was terrible," she murmured, pushing my hands lightly.

I took the hint and moved my arms, freeing up my lap, and she dropped into it, straddling me and wrapping me in her arms.

"I'm sorry," she whispered.

I shuddered.

"I'll be okay," I muttered. "Just hits me hard."

She pressed a kiss to my temple, just above my stitches.

"So...does it hurt now?"

I bit my lip, then started to laugh lightly.

"Yeah, it hurts like a bitch."

Funnily enough, I wasn't sure if I was talking about my head or my heart.

CHAPTER 17

I just want to lay in a pile of warm laundry and eat bread.
-Text from Naomi to Sean

Sean

"Sean."

"Yeah, babe?" I asked, sitting back on my bike and holding it steady with just the power of my legs.

"Have you gotten to the store yet?"

I shook my head. "No. I met a buddy in the parking lot, and we got to BS-ing. What's up?"

I waved my friend off, someone I'd known since high school, and he gave me a two-finger salute before heading inside the grocery store to do his own shopping.

Her voice tremored. "Brady's not here. He's never not here."

My brows rose.

"That's surprising," I admitted. The man was always on time. In fact, he was always early. "Did you call him?"

"Yes," she answered quickly. "I called him about ten times. He's not answering. And I know he didn't forget. He has impeccable timing and remembers everything that I ever say, most of the time using it against me at a later date."

I snorted.

"I'll go check on him, babe," I murmured. "Start your walk. If I find him, I'll send him your way."

"Okay, but if you need to get inside his house, he said there's a key right inside the garage underneath an old golf bag." She blew out a breath. "I don't even know what to do with myself. I feel lost."

"Go walk," I repeated. "I'll call you as soon as I know anything."

"Okay," she breathed. "I love you."

Then she was gone.

I, on the other hand, was finding it hard to breathe.

I love you.

Holy shit.

She'd never once said that to me. Not when I'd just made love to her. Not when I held her in my arms and pressed my lips against her head. Not when we were saying goodbye.

Never.

Then bam.

The words hit me like a sledgehammer, and it took me a few long seconds to get my head unscrambled.

I love you.

Stupidly, I'd been waiting to say those same words to her, unsure if they'd be welcome at this point.

Now that she'd said them, I felt like an asshole for not telling her before now.

As I rode to Brady's place, I realized that I needed to apologize again. She wouldn't think that I needed to, but I did. I'd been holding myself back, even now, because I was too worried that she'd throw the words back in my face.

But she hadn't done that and I should've realized that she wouldn't.

Five minutes later, I pulled into the driveway behind Brady's truck, and turned off the engine.

Everything looked okay from here, even the blinds were open, meaning he was up.

Brows furrowing, I got off the bike, hung my helmet up, and started toward the door that would lead inside from the garage.

I knocked, and waited.

Nothing.

Thirty seconds later, I knocked again.

Nothing.

Worry starting to tighten in my gut, I turned around and walked toward the golf bag, finding the key exactly where she said I'd find it.

Holding the key at the ready, I walked back to the door and tried the knob to find it unlocked and turning in my hand.

Shoving the key into my pocket instead of returning it, I turned the knob fully and pushed the door open.

The minute the door was open, I could hear Butterfinger barking somewhere beyond, and I knocked again, impatient to collect my charge. "Brady! You're late, old man!"

That's when I heard a car pull up.

I backed back out of the house and looked, to find myself unsurprised to see Naomi idling at the curb.

She waved at me apologetically.

I rolled my eyes, turned back to look inside, and called his name again.

I didn't go in yet, though.

Though Brady may be old, he was still likely a good shot, and I didn't want to find my belly full of buckshot.

"Brady!" I shouted. "Yo! My woman is about to lose her shit!"

Still no answer. Butterfinger was going crazy somewhere beyond the kitchen that I could see.

I looked over my shoulder at Naomi who was staring at me through her rolled up window, and shrugged.

She grinned, then mouthed 'go!' to me.

I rolled my eyes, and waited for the shuffle of the man's footsteps, but they never came.

Only the barking, which was getting more and more insistent.

Realizing that something might really be wrong, I stepped over the threshold and stopped in the large, open kitchen area that led straight to the living room.

Although the house was older, it had a ton of potential, and could really become a great place to raise a family. Or had been, according to Brady. He'd raised five kids here, and I could see all the love displayed on the walls, shelves, and hearth.

The kitchen was painted a warm chestnut brown, and the décor obviously leaned more toward old country, which I happened to like.

The living room blended in seamlessly, sporting the same warm brown, and transitioned to a lighter beige about halfway across the room.

The walls were decorated with picture after picture, and in the middle of the fireplace was a large family portrait with seven people, five kids, all very young, and a smiling Brady with his arms around his wife and as many of his kids as he could reach.

He had a smile on a mile wide, and I grinned in reaction to his happiness.

"Brady!" I called again. "You in here?"

It was when I first stepped into the hallway that I got my first hint of something terrible.

I could smell waste, and I worried I was about to walk in on the dog having shit himself because Brady had accidentally left him locked up.

As I started pushing open doors, and looking inside, I quickly realized that this part of the house was empty.

There was one last door to try, and I could practically hear Butterfinger losing it.

"Shit," I sighed.

The dog really did hate me, and I didn't want to open that door.

But I did, and found myself staring down a very angry dog. A dog that was standing over her master with a ferocious snarl on her face.

"Shit," I snapped.

When I tried to step forward though, it was to find Butterfinger getting even more angry.

"Shit!"

I pulled out my phone and dialed 911 even as I was running back outside to Naomi, the only person I knew who Butterfinger actually liked.

"Naomi! Get in here now!" I bellowed at the garage door.

She fell out of her car, and started running toward me even as I got on the phone with EMS.

"I need a medic to 511 Pottersview Road. I have an unconscious male, late eighties early nineties. He's not responsive," I relayed to the operator.

The operator started to ask questions, but I halted them by telling her I knew no more.

She accepted that, and I hung up, running to where I found Naomi trying to get Butterfinger under control.

"Careful, baby," I eased in the room. "She's scared, and I don't want her to hurt you."

Naomi was careful, but luckily Butterfinger was in a willing mood to cooperate, and allowed her close to Brady.

The moment she dropped down to her knees, though, and I heard her soft cry, I realized that Brady wasn't alive anymore.

Not even close.

"Rigor has already set in," she disclosed shakily.

"Can you call the dog off?" I rumbled. "The paramedics will be here shortly, and I don't know if Butterfinger will allow them in."

She swallowed convulsively, and then stood up, calling Butterfinger to her.

"Come here, baby," she called her. "Come to me."

Butterfinger went, but the entire time she kept turning back to look at her master, whimpering with each step she took.

The moment Naomi got her out of the room, I checked for signs of life myself, even though I knew there wouldn't be any of them.

The minute my fingers met the cooled skin of Brady's neck, a deep wave of grief washed over me. Naomi was going to be devastated.

Brady had become one of her greatest friends since moving here, and now that he was gone, she would have a huge hole in her life that he used to fill.

"I put her into my car," Naomi said softly from behind me.

I looked over to her from where I was kneeling beside Brady's body.

"What are you going to do with her?" I asked curiously.

I knew after a discussion a few weeks ago that Naomi wasn't allowed to have dogs at her apartment. The moment she tried to have a dog there, the landlord would kick her out just like she'd done the last four tenants who tried to sneakily have a pet.

"I don't know," she admitted. "But if we take her to the pound, she'll be put down. Everyone will look at her and think she's mean when she's really just heartbroken."

I didn't point out that Butterfinger really was mean. In fact, she was a downright asshole.

Naomi was speaking the truth. If we did take her to the pound, which I knew we weren't, she'd be put down immediately. She was that much of a jerk.

"We'll figure it out in a little bit, baby," I said softly, returning my eyes to the man in front of me. "Gather her food and toys. We'll take her to my place until we figure this out."

With one last glance at Brady's prone body, she turned and escaped.

I stayed there until the medics came through the door, followed on the heels by my father.

"Son," my dad said. "Your woman is in the yard crying next to a dog that growled at me."

My lips twitched.

"Yeah," I said. "She's sad."

Dad took a look at the man, then nodded. "Get out of here. Take your girl home."

Dad clapped his hand on my shoulder to halt me before I could take a step toward the door.

"Did you touch anything?"

Confusion swept over me. "Just touched his body, felt for a pulse, why?"

"Don't touch him."

The two paramedics who were about to bend down froze.

"Get out. Tell my boy outside that we need a crime scene crew."

The two paramedics left just as fast as they came.

"What is it?"

The worry in my voice didn't stop my father from putting his police hat on and ignoring everything about me. "Get out of here, Son."

Aaron came in the room moments later and said, "Crime scene techs have been called. What's wrong?"

That was when my father pointed to a small brass cylinder on the floor.

"Shell casing," he said as he pointed.

My brows lowered in confusion. "That might've just been there," I told him honestly. "He has guns."

Dad proved me wrong by bending down and pushing the side of Brady's head over, revealing a hole in his head right under his ear. "Bullet wound."

"There's no blood," I said. "How the fuck…"

Dad stepped carefully over the carpet, and pushed the door of the bathroom open, and it was there that I saw the blood.

It was everywhere. Splattered on the wall, the floors and even the ceiling. There was blood all the way up to the end of the carpet where it disappeared, but was likely still there we just couldn't see it since the carpet was so dark.

"Why move him?" Aaron asked. "Why not just leave him there."

Before anyone could answer, Brady's phone rang, and dad walked over to the office desk in the corner and pressed the button with a pen that was in his vest pocket.

"Hello?"

Dad looked over at me as he said, "Hi. Who is this?"

The man on the other end of the line laughed like dad had said something hilarious instead of something that was common occurrence when someone called and you wanted to know the person's identity.

"I'm sure you would like to know," the man on the phone said. It was raspy, and so goddamn familiar that I knew that I'd met this guy before somewhere. "You can call me…Mr. Silver."

The man's voice sounded so familiar that my subconscious was practically screaming.

"Hello, Mr. Silver," Dad said. "What can I help you with today."

"I think we can all cut the crap and get to what I really called for," the man that wanted to be called 'Mr. Silver' said silkily. "It's time for you to understand what'll happen if you don't leave her alone."

Dad looked at Aaron in confusion.

"I think that you have us at an advantage," Dad said. "We're confused about what you're talking about."

"You would be, because I'm not actually speaking to you," Silver said. "I'm talking to the man currently standing behind you."

Dad's eyes hit me, and I had a full second to realize that there was a red dot on my chest before I was hit like a linebacker.

The bedroom window glass shattered simultaneously as the wall behind me exploded as something hit it. My entire head throbbed as I hit the ground for the second time in a day.

This time, my head actually did bounce off the floor, but only hard enough for me to see stars instead of it knocking me unconscious.

Ghost lifted up off of me only far enough to stare at me, his face so concerned that he'd accidentally hurt me that it was nearly comical. I hadn't even seen him come in the house.

"Pity," Silver snapped his fingers, the sound reverberating in the room. "Next time, I'll aim better."

I knew that he didn't want to kill me. Had he wanted to kill me, he wouldn't have used a laser. He had to have been standing at the copse of trees just over the property line. He'd have just lined up a shot and taken it before I even knew what hit me.

"Why clean it up?" I croaked.

"I didn't want her to see her friend like that. I felt it prudent to clean him up so the scene wasn't so gruesome."

Then he hung up.

"Where the fuck did you come from?" I groaned. "And goddamn, did you have to hit me so fucking hard?"

Ghost shoved off of me and rolled to the left to avoid the body that was lying on the floor.

"Came to tell you your place was ransacked. Ran by there to pick up the power washer, and found both your dad's place and your trailer a fuckin' mess." He sat up and scooted so his back was to the wall. "Did someone contact the fuckin' cops outside to go look for him yet?"

That was directed at my father, and he jumped as if he'd just been jolted awake.

"Fuck," he rasped, picking up the handheld mic and relaying the message to clear the area.

Once done, he looked at me, was about to say something, and then Naomi ran in. "What in the hell was that?" she gasped, worry outlining her face.

CHAPTER 18

It takes a lot for a man to admit when his woman is wrong.
-Sean's secret thoughts

Sean

"Do you think it was due to his stopping that protest yesterday?" Naomi whispered, pain filling her expression.

I'd just told her about the possibility of it being a murder. Not how I knew, but that my dad suspected it.

I felt terrible for not telling her the rest of what happened after she left. She thought that the window had broken. I didn't tell her that it broke when a bullet, intended for me, came through it.

I didn't want her to worry, not tonight. Not after we found Brady dead. Tomorrow, I'd tell her the truth, but tonight I'd just let her grieve.

This crime, it was angry, yes. But it wasn't something that a group of pissed off college students would perpetrate. What it looked like to me was cold, relentless anger about something, and the perpetrator took it out on the old man because he'd somehow gotten himself on the wrong side of whomever committed this heinous act.

"No, baby," I voiced softly. "I don't think they did it. They've all been accounted for."

I then explained that the protesters hadn't left their post the entire time since we'd left them there the day before other than to run across the street to grab coffee and use the McDonald's facilities before returning.

Her breath hitched.

"This is the shittiest day ever," she replied.

It was and it wasn't.

The sincerity of her words as she told me I love you still shone brightly in the forefront of my mind, despite the terrible stuff that had happened that day.

Her breath hitched again, and I rolled so I could wrap my arms around, pulling her into my chest and dropping my lips down to her head.

"I'm sorry, baby," I murmured against her hair.

The loose strands got tangled in my beard, but I didn't immediately remove them.

I liked the way having her in my arms felt. Loved the way her delicious little body fit perfectly into the curve of mine.

"Make love to me," her voice quivered. "Make me forget this awful day."

"Naomi," I whispered. "We can't do that. Not here. Everyone and their brother is in the clubhouse tonight…Not only will they hear, but it won't make this better."

I placed a kiss on her eyelid and tasted the salty tears that had just started to leak out.

"Please," she whispered.

My heart kicked at the pain in that one word.

"Naomi," I repeated.

Then she kissed me.

My girl went wild in my arms, kissing, licking, caressing.

And I became putty in her hands.

One single kiss was all it took to erase my day. To erase everything horrible that had happened, and turn my focus solely onto the woman in my arms.

"Condom," I said before it got too heated.

She smiled against my lips, knowing that she had me, and rolled.

We were in bed, both of us in nothing but our underwear.

We'd gotten into the bed right after we got out of the shower, and her hair was still wet, the long blonde strands darkened by the dampness.

It fell against my chest, one in particular lashing across my tightened nipple, sending cold tendrils of sensation through my overheated blood.

Her eyes were on me, those beautiful eyes that I thought about non-stop, as she dropped her mouth down to mine, placing one soft kiss on the edge of my lips.

She repeated the process on my nose, eyebrow, jaw, and eyelid before returning to my mouth.

This time I was ready for her, snaking my hands up her back, stopping long enough to unclasp her bra before continuing up her shoulders to curl them around and anchor her to me.

When she tried to give me another soft kiss, I deepened it, licking on the seam of her lips until she opened wide enough that I could push my tongue inside.

"I want to taste you," she breathed, pulling back as far as I would let her.

"You are tasting me," I told her, proving my point by drawing her tongue into my mouth and sucking lightly on it. "Right now."

She pulled back and my eyes fell, taking in the way the tips of her nipples had tightened into stiff peaks.

She saw where my eyes were pointed and moved to brush her chest against mine.

I moaned.

She smiled that teasing smile that I loved, and leaned forward, letting those beautiful breasts hang over my face.

When I went to pull one turgid nipple into my mouth, she put her hand onto my forehead and said, "Stay."

I groaned, let go of her shoulders, and allowed my hands to move to her hips. Once there, I pushed her ass down as my hips came up to meet her, allowing her to feel the hot length of my cock pressed against her core.

She moaned, her eyelids drooping, and as she stared down at me with sex in her eyes.

She lifted up again, separating us, and drug the tip of her nipple along the seam of my mouth.

I opened my mouth, and her nipple grazed the tip of my tongue before she moved again.

She teased me that way for an entire minute, dragging her nipples to my mouth, giving me a single taste before she'd pull away.

By the time she said, "suck" I was already half gone.

I would've rolled, would've taken control, but I sensed she needed this from me right now, the control that I was allowing her to have.

"Push your underwear down," she ordered, eyes glazed over with passion. "I want to feel your cock against me."

It took me less than a second to push my underwear down far enough that my cock was free.

The elastic band was bunched up against my balls, pushing everything up and forcing my cock to sit up straight.

She moaned when the tip of my dick met her ass, and her eyes closed as she lifted up, searched for it with her hand, and laid it down flat so that she could sit on it and work it against her.

"Your panties being off would be better in this situation," I gritted out.

The feel of her hand on my cock was enough to bring me to my knees. Lucky for me I was already on my back.

"Yeah," she agreed. "But I've always had this fantasy…"

My hand went to her hips.

"Yeah?" I urged her to explain. "What fantasy is that?"

She dropped down, allowing the tips of both nipples to play along the dusting of hair on my chest. "To have rough, wild sex. With my panties on, pushed to the side, while I fuck you so hard it hurts inside."

My eyes closed as I played out her fantasy in my head.

The scrape of her panties, sliding along my dick as she took me.

"Yeah," I croaked. "How about you slide those panties over and put me inside?"

She smiled. "I will…but first…"

She moved, dropping down between my thighs.

She shimmied my underwear down my legs, pushing them all the way off until they hung on one toe before returning back up.

I widened my legs for her, allowing her the space she needed.

The moment her mouth hit my cock, my entire body twitched.

The underwear dropped.

And I had to physically force myself not to come undone before she'd even gotten me inside of her mouth.

She'd never done this before. Never taken me into her mouth.

It was probably due to my size. I wasn't a small man, and my cock was proportional to my body.

It intimidated most women, and Naomi was a tiny thing.

That didn't stop her from licking my shaft like a goddamn lollipop though.

Nor rolling my balls around in her hand as she tried to take my entire length into the hot, wet heat of her mouth.

"Fuck me."

That's when she giggled on my cock, sending shivers of impending doom down the backs of my thighs.

"I'm going to come if you don't stop. I'll literally die, right here and now, and you'll be left hanging," I informed her huskily.

Her laugh this time was full and throaty, one she had to pull off of my shaft to do.

"Swear to Christ," I told her, catching hold of her hair as she went back down for more. "I want to be inside of you. I want to fuck you so hard it hurts. Get up here and give me what I need."

She ignored me, instead going back down to take one more slow lick up my shaft before scrambling up my body before settling herself on top of my thighs.

"Hurry," I grunted.

She pushed her panties to the side, giving me my first good look at her pussy since earlier in the morning, and reached backwards for my cock.

The next few seconds were a test of my self-control as she fumbled to get herself situated. She couldn't seem to multitask. When she held her panties to the side, she would raise up, aim my cock for her entrance, and then sit down.

But the first touch of my cock at her entrance had her forgetting what she was doing. Her hand holding her panties to the side twitched, causing her to come to a halt as she tried to gather her panties to the side once again.

She did this three times before I finally took the task into my own hands.

"Hold your panties," I ordered tersely, holding onto my control by a barest fraction of a thread.

She followed my order, pulling them to the side at the same time as I spread her pussy lips.

The new view allowed me to see my cock notched into her entrance.

I held my breath as she started to sink down, her pretty pussy engulfing my cock one slick inch at a time.

When she could go no further, she'd rise back up, then slowly sink back down, taking more with each plunge and retreat.

It was on the seventh stroke that she finally took me fully inside of her.

The moment I was all the way in, she moaned.

"What does it look like?" she breathed, her gasps filling the air around us.

"Like a fucking painting that I'd like to look at each and every day of my life," I grated out. "If you'd let me take a picture and put it as my wallpaper, I'd love you forever."

Her mouth twitched.

"You'd love me forever regardless of whether I did that or not," she countered.

She was right.

I would.

"That's right. I would," I told her. "But that doesn't mean a man can't dream."

Her thighs quivered as she lifted up and let her weight fall back down, as did my balls.

My hands came up to hold onto her sides, just underneath her armpits, my thumb spanning the expanse of ribs that curled around just underneath both breasts.

Her pussy clenched when I swept both thumbs up to lazily sweep across those sensitive buds, and I grunted as I tried to hold my release back. "Ah, fuck."

She grinned, pulled both feet up so they were resting flat right next to my ribs, and said, "Put your hand on my ass and lift me up. I won't be able to do it long if you don't help me."

I did, trying not to stare at her breasts, otherwise I'd come, and fast.

Instead, I settled my eyes on her face, keeping my gaze locked with hers.

The new position forced her to hold onto my arms instead of the seam of her panties, causing them to roughly glide and scrape against my cock with each rise and fall.

My biceps bulged as I lifted her on and off of me. My abdominals clenched as I fought the inevitable climax that bubbled just underneath the surface. Then there was Naomi herself.

Everything about her was so goddamn sexy it hurt. Her eyes. Her hair flying all around her as she moved on me. The way her eyes smoldered as she ran them over me. The flash of her teeth as they sunk into her bottom lip as she came down on my cock.

My eyes dropped when I felt her hand where we were joined, and I watched as she gathered some of the wetness that was accumulating at the base where we were connected.

The moment her fingers were fully coated in that wetness, she brought those same fingers up to circle around the delicate skin of her clit.

My hands clenched deeply into her ass, likely leaving imprints of my fingers behind. If she made me hold off any longer, those marks would turn to bruises.

The tips of both my pointer fingers fell into the crack of her ass, the tips brushing over that little puckered entrance.

When that accidental brush happened, she detonated.

One second she was lingering, trying to draw out the orgasm that we were both chasing, and the next she was coming so hard that I saw stars.

No longer able to hold on, I let go and came fast and almost violently inside of her.

And it took just seconds for me to realize that the condom I'd asked her to fetch was still on my chest between us. Yet, neither one of us had paused long enough in our activities to put it on.

I couldn't stop myself though. Even knowing that I was possibly putting both of us at risk of becoming parents at this point was enough to cause my cock to harden impossibly further.

Her breathing was ragged, and mine didn't sound much better.

Being in really great shape didn't automatically mean that you wouldn't lose your breath when your brain was solely focused on the feeling of the pussy that was sucking every drop of cum out of the tip of your dick.

I wasn't a liar, and I wasn't one to beat around the bush.

"You take my breath away," I whispered fiercely to her. "You make me want to be a better man. A man who you can always count on to never let you falter."

Her head came up, and I realized who it was I was dealing with in a matter of seconds.

My other half. The compliment to my soul.

"The same goes for you," she murmured fiercely. "It physically hurts to think about being away from you, and it scares the crap out of me that one day you might not be here for me anymore."

I rolled us over, my elbows resting in the bed on either side of her head, as my cock slid out from her to rest wetly against the seam of her sex.

"I won't ever be far," I promised her. "And even if I am, all you have to do is call. I'll come back to you the moment I hear you need me. I love you. I've loved you for a while, and I've been so scared to tell you."

Her eyes watered.

The moment she came down from her high, I waited for it to start.

And she didn't disappoint.

The instant everything came back, she was crying again.

And there wasn't a damn thing I could do about it.

***

"Come," I ordered, standing up and rummaging through my drawers.

I couldn't watch her sit on that couch and cry for another minute longer.

"Why?" she sniffled. "I don't want to get up."

I found some socks, slipped them onto my large feet, and then slipped said large feet into my tennis shoes that I work to work out in.

Once I got my feet into my shoes, I nabbed another pair of socks and walked over to Naomi. I reached for her leg and pulled the socks into place.

They fit her loosely, going all the way up to just below her knee.

"Don't ask me why," I said. "Get up. Go pee. Get your shoes on. In that order."

She shot me a glare.

"There's nothing you can do at this point to make the hurt go away," she informed me as she rose. "I'll be better if you just leave me be."

I grabbed her shoes and held them up for her.

She still didn't move.

"If you make me start counting like I do with kids, you're not going to like what I do to you."

She snorted as she reached for her shoes, surprising me when she actually put them on and stood up with expectation lighting her eyes.

"Where to, Seanshine?"

I frowned at her. Hard.

"Why do you insist on calling me that?" I asked casually, not letting on that I absolutely hated that name.

Why my father, friends, and colleagues insisted on calling me that, was beyond me. Even when they knew how much I hated it.

"Your friend, Memphis, calls you that."

My brows rose.

"When did you have a chance to talk to Memphis?" I asked in surprise.

Her lips tipped up at the corners. "When she called and I answered your phone while you were in the shower earlier. I now have lots and lots of ammo to use against you the next time we fight."

My frown was likely ferocious.

"Whatever she told you, you can't believe," I informed her. "Trust me. She's the devil."

I picked up the two gloves in the corner and turned to her, holding them up in my hands.

"That'll never fit me," she informed me.

I shrugged.

"It'll be all right," I promised. "I'll even let you use mine, which is smaller."

And that's how I hit my girlfriend with a baseball, giving her a black eye. Luckily, I wasn't throwing the ball like I would have in a real game or it could have been a lot worse.

The smile she gave me, though...that was worth every second of guilt that the bruise on that beautiful face gave me.

CHAPTER 19

You look like the type of woman who has to buy her own Klondike bars.
-E-card

Sean

"The fucking dog hates me, too," I grumbled. "I walk into my own goddamned trailer, and she growls at me."

My dad had the fucking nerve to laugh.

"That's sad," he lied. "I think she's kind of cute."

In an ugly kind of way, I suppose you could say that.

"Did you at least get the beer?"

I glared at my father and tossed him the thirty-six pack.

He grunted as he caught it, and I tried really hard not to laugh.

"Where's Naomi?"

"Inside talking to the ladies," I answered.

Ghost came up behind me, and I froze at the look on his face.

"You okay?"

A few weeks ago, when he'd asked me to go with him to do

something, never in a thousand years would I have thought that I'd see what I saw. I had no earthly idea that he would ask me to do what he did. To make me witness something so fucking heartbreaking that I couldn't stop thinking about it, even now.

Right that second, seeing that look on his face, the raw, naked fear, I straightened, remembering that night like it was as clear as day.

"Ghost."

"I'm going to tell you something, and I want you to promise me that it'll never, ever get out. If you tell anyone, even that woman of yours, it could be the death of them."

***

Four weeks ago

"I'm going to tell you something, and I want you to promise me that it'll never, ever get out. If you tell, even that woman of yours, it could be the death of them."

"Are you sure you want to go?" I asked raggedly.

Ghost stared at the crying little girl, the one with tears pouring down her cheeks as she stared at her mother like she'd just betrayed her. The one with the two French braids that started at the top of her head and fell to almost mid back...hair the same color as the man who was standing next to me. Her eyes were the same color, too. Deep green, almost the color of an olive, with whiskey colored striations that broke that green up beautifully.

"I hate you!" the little girl screamed.

The woman, she was beautiful. She had long brown hair that fell in waves to nearly her waist, and the most soulful brown eyes that looked like they'd literally been poured from melted chocolate.

"Sweetheart," the woman whispered. "Please."

"It's not okay. It'll never be okay. He's not my father. I'm not ever going to call him daddy. I only ever had one, and he's gone. You

don't get to decide that for me!"

My heart shattered into a million pieces, especially when I saw the murderous rage that was filling Ghost's frame.

"He didn't ask you to call him daddy..."

"Let's go."

I followed Ghost, but not far.

He went to the house next door just a mere house length away from the two ladies that were loving a Ghost, and knocked on the door.

The man who we'd seen leaving the house where the little girl and her mother lived only five minutes before opened the door and stared at Ghost. "Who're you?"

"You're going to move."

The man's eyebrows rose. He was tall, a little less than six feet, with brown hair the color of muddy water, and blue eyes that looked way too light to be real. His teeth were so fucking white and straight that it was obvious that they were fake, and to top it all off, his voice was too high. He sounded like a woman.

"Yeah?"

His smile was slick, oily. And I wanted to beat it off him, and I didn't even know what the fuck was going on.

"Yeah," Ghost confirmed. "I don't care where you go, or what you do, but you're no longer going to live here."

"How do you know that?" the man crossed his arms over his chest.

Ghost pulled out some papers from his pocket.

"You're being evicted."

Ghost handed the papers to the man, and the man took them.

"You can't kick me out. You're not my landlord."

Ghost's smile was scary.

"Yes, I am," he interjected. "And you have exactly twenty-four hours, per the contract, to move your shit and get out before I seize all assets left in the house and burn them."

The man's smile looked a little brittle.

"There's a house across the street," the man said. "I'll just move in there."

Ghost's smile got even scarier.

"I own every goddamn house on this block, and trust me, you won't be renting any of them."

The man stiffened.

"You have no right."

Ghost took a step forward, pressed his face forward until only inches separated him from the man, and said something so softly that I could barely hear it. "You did the wrong thing tonight. I'll let you figure out what it was."

Then we were leaving, walking back down the street to where we'd left the bikes.

"Ghost, what the hell is going on?"

***

Ghost looked sick.

"I need to ride somewhere and I need all of you to go with me."

Aaron, Truth, Tommy Tom, Jessie, Fender, my father and I all stared.

"Whatever you need, man. And we're there," Tommy Tom was the one who spoke.

"We'll stay back with the ladies. You go ahead and do what you need to do," Fender pointed to Jessie.

Jessie who looked so distracted that I almost said no, that someone else needed to stay.

His eyes were all for Ellen, and I wondered if I was going to have to give them permission or something to get him to take his foot out of his ass and make a move.

The urgency in Ghost's tone had us all moving toward the house where the ladies were gabbing, all of us peeling off toward our respective women as we explained what was going on.

"Sean," Naomi sat forward, her hand holding a glass of wine. "What's wrong?"

"There's something wrong with Ghost, and I'm riding with him. I want you to stay in the clubhouse tonight with the other ladies. We're going to be gone for at least twelve hours," I informed her. "I'd appreciate it if you called into work for the both of us."

Because if we were going where I guessed we were going, then it'd be at least twelve hours. Six there, and six back. And there was no telling what we were about to walk into.

"That's fine," she said. "We just got the new sheets for your room."

We did.

Naomi had stayed there only once when she declared that she wouldn't stay there again until there were new sheets, new pillows, curtains covering the windows and toilet paper in the bathroom that didn't look like it came from the Super Supply Store that only carried industrial strength.

"You wouldn't know what it feels like to wipe your vagina with something so rough, but trust me. It sucks."

Grinning at the memory, I nodded my head. "Yeah, we did."

"I'll be okay. I don't plan on walking in front of the windows naked, so I'll be fine for tonight. Is there anything you need us to do?"

I shook my head.

"No," I amended. "Not yet, at least."

With that I placed one single kiss on the tip of her nose—anything more would make my cock hard, and that would suck to ride with for six hours straight—with the rest of the club at my back.

"We're ready," Tommy Tom said. "What do you want us to do?"

That was the good thing about a club. They had your back, with no questions asked.

One of our own called, and we dropped everything to make sure he didn't have to face shit alone.

CHAPTER 20

If you have to talk out of your ass, at least stand up. I simply cannot tolerate mumbling.
-E-card

Naomi

I was staring at the door, wondering what in the hell I was doing.

The clubhouse was full—of women.

Only two men remained, Fender, a man I hadn't gotten to know that well yet, but he seemed nice. And then there was Jessie James. Jessie, I really didn't know, but that was in deference to my man. I didn't want Sean to think I was trying to make friends with him. Especially not after his previous girlfriend left him for Jessie.

Really, I wanted to be anywhere but here right now, especially with what had been going on behind my closed door for the last thirteen minutes and thirty-three seconds.

I knew the exact time because I'd been lying in bed, staring at the clock, wondering when Sean would call and let me know that he was all right when the party had started.

Well, I called it a party…Ellen and Jessie might call it a 'fight.'

To-may-toe, to-mah-toe and all that fun shit.

"Seriously, it's like you don't even care," Ellen hissed. "You don't care what kind of a mess you left me in ten years ago. All you care about is your own fucking self. You don't even have the balls to pursue me. I left Sean for you. I liked Sean. But the minute you showed up, my whole freakin' world changed. I couldn't lie to Sean. I couldn't continue to live that lie. I've loved you since we were freshmen in high school. That's fifteen years, Jessie!"

Whoa. There was more to this than met the eye.

"You don't think I know that, Ellie?" Jessie countered. "You don't think that was the hardest decision of my life? Because, let me just tell you something. It was. I regret that mistake every single second that I fucking breathe. Seeing you that first day I pledged to the club, it broke me. I was holding on by a thread, and there you come, waltzing right back into my life when I was barely breathing to begin with."

That was deep. Really deep.

And it sucked, because I was beginning to feel sorry for the two of them. Before, I'd hated them on principle, and now I was literally on the edge of the fence, leaning heavily toward sorrow and pity for the two people that had known each other in another life. One before Sean.

Jessie had obviously been *in there* with his 'Ellie' way before even Sean realized.

Poor guy never stood a chance.

Not that I was complaining.

If he had, I wouldn't be in his bed right now, curled around his pillow and wearing his t-shirt because it smelled like him.

My phone buzzed, and I looked down, grimacing when I saw that it was work.

Again.

Shit.

"Hello?" I answered.

"If either you or Sean don't come in tonight, you're both fired."

That was my boss, Steve. Good ol' Steve.

"I already told you that we're both down with food poisoning," I lied for the second time that night.

Steve was a bastard. There was no fucking way in the world he would've just accepted 'we're not coming in.' He would need a good excuse, and if it wasn't good, then we'd both be docked points. And we were only allowed fifteen points before we were up for review. And if we accrued any more while we were under 'review' then there was the option that we may be fired.

It was bullshit, and something that sucked, but it was what it was.

"I'm sorry, Steve," I started to say, but stopped when he interrupted me.

"Cline and Maran were in an accident. Medic six is totaled. We need someone here, and it doesn't matter if you're throwing up. It's only in the worst-case scenario that we'll use the medic we're putting you on. It's the backup's backup, and something we don't want to use unless it's absolutely necessary."

"Shit," I whispered under my breath. "Sean can't come. He's too sick, but I can be there in about half an hour."

If I pushed it.

I'd have to borrow one of the girl's cars, or have them take me.

Either way, I wasn't going to leave him hanging.

"Are Cline and Maran okay?" I asked worriedly.

"Yes," he said. "Shaken up. Cline has a few possible broken ribs, and Maran has a seatbelt bruise, but it could've been worse."

Yes, it could have. I'd been in something much worse when at the Kilgore Fire Department that had almost killed me while I was working an accident as a student paramedic.

PD had saved me. If he hadn't, I'd have been a flattened pancake who never had to worry about anything again.

"You paying attention, woman, or do I need to fire you?"

I gritted my teeth.

"I'll be there."

Then I hung up, because I didn't like talking to Steve. Steve was a douche on a good day. Today, he was a used douche.

One that I couldn't stand and who Sean couldn't either.

Sighing, I got up and walked to the small overnight bag that I'd left here two weeks ago and dug inside, unearthing a pair of my work pants, a white wife beater, and a white shirt.

I was dressed for work, I opened my door as quietly as I could, thankful that nobody realized what I was doing. Because if they had, they definitely would've stopped me.

Ellen's dejected face was the first thing I saw as she headed for the door, and I stopped her by calling her name quietly.

"Ellen."

She froze, looking at me with tears in her eyes, and smiled sadly.

"Yeah?"

"Do you think you could take me to work?"

She eyed my clothes, then nodded as one single tear slipped down her cheek.

"Yes, I think I can manage that before I go."

"Go?" I asked as I came up to her side.

She didn't reply, she just opened the door and headed outside to her car.

She pulled open the door on her side, then popped the trunk.

"There's not much room in the back," she said as she did. "It's full of clothes and stuff."

I stowed my stuff in the trunk, but didn't comment about the boxes I could see packed in the back.

Instead, I walked around to the passenger door and dropped inside before giving her directions to my work.

She started driving, and the silence started to grow.

I let my mind wander, not wanting to care about this woman, but finding it increasingly harder not to do so.

I'd started making grocery lists in my head. When I got to dog food, I froze.

"Shit, shit, shit, shit, shit," I groaned. "Could we please go by Sean's place? I left Butterfinger all by herself, and she needs to go out or she'll pee all over the place, and then Sean will have a reason to get rid of her."

Ellen's mouth twitched.

"Yeah, I can do that."

We pulled into the driveway, and Ellen came to a stop next to Sean's truck.

I grinned.

"I'll take Sean's truck," I said. "Since we're here now and all. You don't have to wait."

Ellen smiled.

"Sean wouldn't let me drive his truck, you know."

My brows rose in surprise. I drove his truck whenever the hell I felt like it, and he didn't give a shit.

"Because he didn't want you to, or because you didn't want to?" I questioned.

Her look was unreadable.

"You got in there way deeper than I ever did," she said softly. "And likely that was because I was already guarding my heart because of Jessie. Whatever the reason, I'm glad he found you. You two seem great together, and he deserves something fantastic."

With that, she put the car in reverse and backed out of the driveway, leaving me there to contemplate the hatred that was quickly dissipating toward her.

Shaking my head, I jogged up to the house, where I could already hear Butterfinger barking, and tapped in the key code on the garage door, causing it to open.

I'd just placed my hand on the door knob and pushed it open when something hit me from behind. Something hard. Something so hard that I saw stars in the backs of my eyes.

I crumpled to the ground, and Butterfinger came barreling out the door so fast and stealthily that the attacker who was in the process of hitting me again never saw her coming.

The man cursed.

CHAPTER 21

Boobs are my favorite part of the day.
-Sean's secret thoughts

Sean

"What do you mean she left?" I growled. "You were supposed to keep all the women there at the clubhouse."

"I didn't know she left. I was using the bathroom. Came back in to find Ellen gone. Didn't think to even look for Naomi until thirty minutes later when she didn't come down for the game the girls wanted to play with her."

"Did you check my place?"

Jessie grunted. "On the way there now. Though the cops might beat me there."

"How long has she been gone?" I asked. "Who took her?"

"Ellen."

One word had the power to make anger ignite in my blood.

"And who the fuck told Ellen she could leave?"

Jessie didn't say anything for a really long moment, and I knew

241

without confirmation that he was the one who caused her to leave.

"She and I had a fight. She left when I was in the bathroom."

"Jesus Christ," I hissed. "Find out where she is and call me back."

I turned back around, realizing that I now had the attention of all the men at my side.

"What's wrong?" Ghost rasped.

He was edgy and twitching. And he was acting fucking wired, like something was about to happen that might very well change his life.

"Naomi left with Ellen, and Jessie can't find her."

"Well fuck," Dad growled. "Do you want to turn around?"

I shook my head.

"No."

Though I was worried, I didn't think it necessary to leave yet. We'd made good time to Louisiana, and now that we were here, I wanted to see whatever was broken that Ghost needed fixed.

But when we arrived at the house, it was to find it entirely empty. No lights. No stuff. No car…no nothing.

The house that had been so full of life a few weeks ago was now an empty shell. There was nothing there. Not even any trash.

"Fuck, fuck, FUCK!" Ghost yelled.

My eyes widened, and my gaze connected with Truth's.

Something passed between us, and I now realized that I had someone beside me who was just as worried about the man as I was.

Fucking perfect.

As if I wasn't aware things could get any worse, my phone rang, pulling me back into the present.

Fishing the phone out of my pocket, I placed it to my ear and said, "Hello?"

"Fuck, man. There's blood all over your garage. I haven't been into the house yet, but it's bad. You need to come back."

It's bad. You need to come back.

Those words echoed in my head for the next six hours.

I didn't stop. Not even for gas, which I needed.

Badly.

I was running on fumes as I pulled into the parking lot of the hospital.

For expedience, I drove right up to the ambulance bay, parked my bike on the sidewalk that led to it, and sprinted inside.

I'd gotten a call about thirty minutes in that had told me that Naomi had been found inside the house with the damn dog that hated me.

Lucky for us that Naomi was aware long enough to get Butterfinger to calm the fuck down, or they would've had to tranquilize her to get her to stop protecting Naomi.

The moment I made it into the ER, I was directed to a room by two nurses who knew exactly who I was. It was odd being on this end of the spectrum rather than being the one who gave the directions and information on a patient.

"She's in three."

I nodded at Rainey, one of the nurses and then walked to the curtained off area. The only curtain that was closed in the entire ER.

The soft fabric of the curtain felt rough in my hands as I pushed it back slowly, and what I saw took my breath away.

I bent over, my hands on my knees, as I tried to breathe to stop the vomit that threatened to rise up my throat.

"Seanshine."

Her rasping voice had me straightening, and I walked on stiff legs toward the bed where Naomi was looking at me through one swollen eye.

The other was swollen shut, and she was likely unable to open it at all.

"Hey, baby," I rasped.

"I'm fired."

I blinked.

"Okay," I said. "Why?"

I was trying to follow her train of thought, but all I could think about was the way her face and every inch of skin I could see was a smattering of black, blue, and purple.

Even her fingers were bruised.

And those fingers also were missing fingernails.

The nausea grew.

"Our lovely boss called and told me that the crew that took over for us was in an accident. That either I came in or we were both fired."

My mouth thinned at her rasped words, and I wanted to kill that mother fucker. *Slowly, with my bare hands.*

"And you went in?" I guessed.

That had to be the reason she left.

"Yeah," she nodded, swallowing hard when the movement caused something to hurt.

Likely everything.

She was quiet for a long minute while she composed herself, and then she turned and looked at me with apologetic eyes.

"I didn't mean to do this."

I moved, placing one hand on the side of her face. My fingertips barely grazed her hair, and she moved her cheek into my palm despite it having to hurt.

"I know you didn't mean to do it, baby," I said. "I'm just glad you're okay."

"Butterfinger saved me."

I knew that.

"Guess she's allowed to stay."

A quiet laugh left Naomi's lips, and then the curtain was drawn aside.

"Sean."

I turned to find Tommy Tom, doctor's coat on over his fucking blue jeans, standing next to another doctor who was new and who I hadn't had the chance to become acquainted with.

"Yeah?" I asked.

He gestured for me to come out while a nurse took my spot.

"She's going to give Naomi some more meds to get her settled down and resting comfortably. She apparently refused anything until you arrived so she could speak to you coherently."

That made my gut knot.

It also sounded exactly like something she'd say and do.

The minute I was out of earshot, Tommy Tom gestured to the

doctor at his side. "This is Dr. Mishvele."

I nodded at him.

"She's fine."

My brows rose.

He held up his hand.

"Despite the bruises, we believe that nothing is broken. She has some broken skin on her hands that were likely defensive wounds. The baby is all right, though we're monitoring that closely just in case…"

His words were lost on me as the words 'the baby' replayed over and over through my head.

Tommy Tom, realizing I'd zoned out, smiled a knowing smile, and held his hand up for Mishvele to stop.

"How do you know about the baby so Sean here can get his head wrapped around it? By the look on his face, it's likely he didn't know about the baby."

Mishvele's eyebrows lifted. "Blood tests confirm. Based on the hormone levels in her blood, I'm assuming she's at least eight weeks, if not more, along."

My mouth dropped open.

That would mean that it had to be the very first time we had sex that she conceived.

At least that time we'd worn condoms.

Jesus.

"Okay."

I was so fucking dumbfounded.

Had Naomi known?

I immediately shook that thought off. No, she hadn't known. If she had, I would've known.

"Other than the outward appearance, she was a very lucky woman."

Lucky…yeah, if you wanted to call getting beaten black and blue lucky.

"Thank you, Dr. Mishvele. Are they going to be moving her out of the ER soon?"

He nodded, then rattled off a room number in a unit two floors up.

Woodenly, I walked back into the room and dropped down on the side of Naomi's bed as carefully as I could so I wouldn't disturb her sleep.

Then I stared at her for a few long minutes, my mind going a hundred miles an hour.

It was about twenty minutes later that I was kicked out so she could be moved, and since she was going to a floor that didn't allow visitors except during visiting hours, I wasn't allowed to go with her until they got her settled into her room.

Meaning I had time to fume.

CHAPTER 22

I don't like who I become when left alone with a bag of Butterfinger minis.
-Sean's secret thoughts

Sean

I looked down at my woman.

She looked so broken. Bruised and hurt.

She was so still. I hadn't heard her voice since she'd been moved, and I wanted to so badly I could taste it.

I wanted to scream.

I wanted to cry out, yell about the injustice of it all.

I didn't, though.

Instead, I calmly bent down and placed a kiss on the one area of Naomi's cheek that wasn't covered in ugly purple bruises before I turned and walked out.

My hands were fisted at my sides, and with each step that I took, my adrenaline started pumping.

I made it into the hallway and looked down the hall at the waiting room.

Ellen was crying softly with her arms wrapped around her upraised knees, but I couldn't find it in me to apologize for the awful words that I'd said to her when she came up to me and tried to apologize.

Jessie was sitting on Ellen's right, jaw clenched and just as pissed off now as he had been when I arrived at the hospital and started spewing my mouth at the woman we all knew he loved but wasn't acting on it.

The moment he saw me emerge, he got up, patted Ellen awkwardly on the head, and headed toward us.

Ellen shot daggers at his back, her eyes shooting invisible death rays at his retreating form as he made his way toward us.

"Blood trail leads down the street," Jessie recounted, breaking into the silence. "I followed it. Leads to an empty house, a house that it looks like it's been squatted in for a while. He cleaned himself up in the bathroom with an emergency first aid kit that was still out on the counter. We got DNA. Sent it to the lab."

"They expedite it for me like I asked?" Dad asked.

Jessie nodded. "Yeah. I also have a grainy photo that some woman took while she was walking her dog. It's not much, but it's something."

Jessie showed me the photo, and I cursed. We couldn't do anything with that.

"Hold on," I said. "Can you forward that to an email?"

Jessie nodded.

I rattled off the email and then placed a call.

Though it was late at night, Jack answered, and he didn't even sound pissed.

"Yo," he sounded like he was awake.

"Jack, I sent you an email of a picture. I know you're not as good with the photos, but I was hoping you could talk your wife into taking a look at it," I swallowed. "My woman was attacked by this man tonight, and I need to know who it is so I can look for him."

Jack said something that wasn't to me, and suddenly I heard his wife say, "I got it. Give me five."

Jack relayed the message, even though I heard what she said.

"Thanks."

I hung up.

And waited.

And waited.

And waited.

My hands clenched and unclenched while the men around me spoke. They all offered ideas on where to look, offered to search the surrounding hospitals and clinics in the area, but I knew it wouldn't be enough.

I needed more.

And Jack's wife didn't disappoint.

My phone rang five minutes and thirty-seven seconds later. I pulled it out of my pocket and answered it with barely disguised anguish.

"Pulled the pic. Ran it through the database. Man's name is Walton Whitley. Goes by the name 2W. Forty-seven. Member of a motorcycle club that is based out of Corpus Christi, Texas," Jack said without preamble. "I pulled up a photo of the man from a news article, and he was standing next to a biker who wrecked a few months ago on the way to a smokehouse. I'm sending you everything I have on him. He also used his credit card at an ATM on the outskirts of Mooresville about thirty minutes ago."

The minute those words were said, I knew exactly who it was without seeing the photo. Things started to fit into place as I finally solved the puzzle. Too late, but I'd solved it.

"Thanks, man," I grated out. "I'll owe that wife of yours a hug."

Jack snorted. "No. I'll give her the hug and say it's from you."

I laughed darkly and hung up, then turned to the men of my club who were waiting for the news right along with me.

They'd be scouring the street if I thought it'd help, but they were waiting for direction on my end before they started.

"Walton Whitley or 2W. Ring any bells?"

My father was the one to answer.

"No." He shook his head. "But the fact that you're so calm right now tells me that you do."

He was right.

When things got confusing or complicated, I centered myself.

I never, ever went off halfcocked. I thought everything through before I did it, and prided myself on the fact.

Right now, though, the need to tear this man apart with my bare hands for what he did to my woman was almost overwhelming me, and it took a lot for me to try to calm myself enough to fill my club brothers in on what I'd learned.

The only reason I wasn't was because we were in the hospital hallway right outside Naomi's room.

"You remember that guy that I nearly got into a fight with at the smokehouse a few months back?" I asked. "The one that was looking at Naomi? Touching her?"

The moment I mentioned that, their confusion clouded.

"It does look like him," Jessie voiced. "I can definitely see it now."

"The ambulance that was in the accident was caused by a

motorcycle."

I looked up to find my father, staring at me, understanding dawning in his eyes. I knew it, I knew in my gut that it was him. He'd orchestrated all of this. He'd known we'd left. He knew, because he'd been watching her for weeks. Maybe even longer. Likely since he'd seen her at the smokehouse all those weeks ago.

"It was him," I reported, knowing it was the truth without even having it confirmed. "He did it so she would go."

My father nodded his head in understanding.

"They said he was last seen at the ATM on Center Street about thirty minutes ago. Knowing Jack, he's already emailed out the make and model of the bike. Though, in this town, it'll be easy to find him."

A foreign bike in the Rejects territory would stick out like a sore thumb.

This area was the Dixie Wardens' territory, and we didn't tolerate any other bikers causing disruptions in our town.

And that's what this man had done. He'd taken that safe place away from Naomi, and I wouldn't tolerate it.

Pulling my phone out, I forwarded the email to all of the men, and then looked at Jessie.

"You think you can stay with them?"

He seemed to draw a deep breath, thankful that I still trusted him with my woman's life.

It wasn't his fault that this had happened, and I knew that.

Rationally, anyway.

In my heart, I was still pissed off at him.

"I'll stay with them."

'Them' being Ellen, Imogen, Tally and Verity who were all holed up in the waiting room hoping to visit with Naomi once we'd gone.

I looked up to find Ghost.

My heart kicked at seeing him.

We'd left him in Benton, staring at the house where his woman had been not a few weeks before.

"Thanks, man."

Ghost's eyes were dead.

"When this is done, you're next."

Ghost blinked, shuddered, and then nodded once.

"Yeah," he agreed. "It's time."

It was. It was time for all of us to be happy, and once I found the stupid son of a bitch who'd hurt Naomi, I would set Jack on finding his woman and kid, too.

***

We all rode out, except Ghost, each of us taking a different direction as we headed further away from the property.

"Got a BOLO on him."

My father's words as we left did nothing to alleviate my fears. Visions of Naomi's face and thoughts of the tiny little life that I hadn't even known about that was nearly taken from me were enough to make my entire body vibrate with barely concealed fury.

The BOLO—or be on the lookout—wasn't going to be enough. I wasn't sure that having the three cops who were on duty at the time on the lookout for a motorcycle was really going to help. Not at this point.

The man was probably hiding away somewhere, trying to recover.

None of the hospitals or clinics we'd checked had seen him, which meant either he wasn't getting treated for his injuries—injuries I knew he had thanks to Naomi waking up and telling me what little she was able to tell me before she fell back to sleep—or he was getting treated privately.

Luckily, the local news stations were running the story about the countywide manhunt for the piece of shit, so we weren't the only eyes on the road that night.

But as minutes turned to hours and those hours multiplied, I knew it was time for more drastic measures.

I'd just decided to call Jack back to see what else he could come up with, when the shine off of some chrome caught my eyes in the darkened alley next to the old emergency animal hospital.

Since the animal hospital had closed down over a year and a half ago, I knew that nothing should be over there, let alone something so shiny. So, whatever it was probably wasn't supposed to be there.

Thinking I was chasing a crazy trail of hope, I pulled my bike over a block away and walked toward the alley.

The moment I breached the alley's entrance, I realized that my imagination hadn't been messing with me. The flash of something shiny that I'd seen out of the corner of my eye had actually been the spokes of a motorcycle. One that I'd seen twice. Once when I'd pulled into the parking lot of the smokehouse, and another time when we all pulled over to check on the motorcyclist who had gone down and had died.

It was distinctive. The rim of the tire was fuckin' huge, and had to be uncomfortable to ride on with the sheer magnitude of the wheel and the tire itself.

I found my phone without any conscious thought and was already calling my father back as I made my way further into the alley.

There were four doors, two leading into the vacant former animal hospital, and two leading into an old furniture store that I was surprised hadn't closed down right along with the animal hospital.

"You found something?" my father asked into my ear.

"At the old animal hospital on Tuttle," I murmured quietly into my phone. "The doors to the hospital are open, as are the ones to the furniture place."

"Give us five, and we'll check out both together."

I didn't wait.

I walked straight into the old hospital, and flipped the tactical light on at the end of my H&K forty-five.

The gun felt comfortable in my hand, and somehow, I was able to maneuver throughout the building without my heart racing.

I wanted this guy to know pain, I wanted him to feel some at my hands. I wanted him to suffer, day in and day out, for the rest of his natural born life. I wanted his experience in prison to be hell on earth and for some big guy to violate him in the shower. I wanted his parole denied each and every time it came up, dashing his hopes and leaving him a broken man.

I wanted him to be a shell of a man, but I wanted him to live. I wanted him to have a front row seat to the shithole his life was going to be once I got finished with him.

And I was confident that I would be able to make all of that happen for him.

I knew a lot of people. Some good and some bad. And each and every one of them would help me with what I wanted to accomplish when it came to this guy's quality of life for the rest of his years on this planet.

I didn't care how many favors I had to pull. I'd pull every last one of those mother fuckers until I had nothing left to pull.

A sound at my back had me freezing, and just when I was about to aim my gun behind me, Tommy Tom, still in his goddamn scrubs, came up behind me. He had a gun similar to my own in his hand, and he was an altogether different man than the one I'd seen in the hospital telling me I was going to be a father.

This one was lethal. He was scary. He was my brother, and I was glad to have him at my back.

"Your father and Truth are in the furniture store checking it out. If I had to guess, this is the one I'd say he was in."

That was my guess, too.

Maybe they left something behind, and…I froze, staring at the body lying on the floor.

"Surely, it can't be that easy," Tommy Tom rumbled from behind me. At my six.

"You took the words right out of my goddamn mouth," I murmured. "Cover me."

Tommy Tom shifted, covering our backs, as he watched me approach the body.

It took less than thirty seconds to confirm that this man was the Walton character I'd seen at the smokehouse. The same one who we were ninety-nine percent positive was the man responsible for assaulting Naomi.

"He's out," I said, categorizing the shit laying around him in a heartbeat. Drugs, painkillers in particular, littered the floor. Saline. Gauze. Betadine. Alcohol. Syringes.

I lifted my foot and kicked the man's shoulder, causing him to moan and roll onto his back. His face was just as fucked up as the body parts I could see.

And that's when I had my suspicions confirmed. "Dog bites on his face. Arms. Chest. Likely some on his legs, too, but it doesn't look like he got that far before he passed out."

Tommy Tom relayed the message to my father and the men that had followed him, and it wasn't two minutes later that they all arrived.

Each of us surrounded the man.

"Seems anti-climactic."

That was said by Aaron, and Truth snorted.

"We don't always have to have shoot outs and car wrecks," Aaron laughed under his breath. "This is actually damn nice. No getting shot at…"

A gunshot rang out, and that was when I realized that he must have pulled a gun, because he was trying with all his might to raise it up and aim for me.

He only succeeded in getting it up about an inch off the floor before it fell again.

"You were saying?" I drawled, taking a step forward and placing my booted foot over the man's wrist and then pressing down with the majority of my weight.

We ignored his whimpering cries, and I twisted my foot viciously, extremely satisfied with the way his wrist snapped.

"Dog bites are funny things," Tommy Tom said, bending down to examine the cuts. "It's crazy how infected they can get."

He picked up a pipe, rusted and covered in something that I couldn't make out, and drug it across the man's wounds on his arms, ensuring that he would get an infection.

The lacerations were seeping with blood, and I had to force myself not to pick the pipe up and whack the man across the head with it.

He deserved it, but the wounds needed to coincide with the dog bites. If I added any more to them that didn't fit, others might grow suspicious, and there was no way in hell I was implicating myself in this.

I wasn't stooping down to that level.

I had really good intentions, too.

I was going to walk away. I was going to give the man over to my father, the police chief. I was going to go back to that hospital. Force myself to stay away from him until he was in the care of the Mooresville Jail System.

That all flew out the window when the man grinned at me.

"Was gonna enjoy taking your woman."

My eyes dropped to the man on the floor.

He was laying on the floor, broken and bleeding, and yet he still had a fuckin' mouth on him.

He was surrounded by six men who would like nothing better than to separate his face from his body, yet he still had the balls to say words that he knew would piss them off.

I smiled.

Then I kicked him in the face, ensuring he wouldn't be talking any time soon.

Mainly because he had a broken jaw, and likely he would need reconstructive surgery to put it back together again.

"That's enough," my father said. "If you fuck him up anymore, I'll have to do reports, and you know how much I hate paperwork."

I walked off without another word, and went to the hospital where my woman waited.

***

"I don't want him next to my woman," I growled at the doctor. "I don't care how critical he is. You either get him gone off this fuckin' floor, or I'm taking my woman somewhere she'll feel safe."

"Sean," my father started.

I turned and gave my father a look that he couldn't misconstrue.

"No," I seethed. "She's not going to continue to feel scared. She deserves to be somewhere that's going to give her that sense of calm she needs to heal."

My father held up a hand. "What about moving him to the room I saw closest to the nurses' station? That way he still has the medical attention he needs, but he's not so close to her as to cause her any worry." He hesitated. "You want the man healthy, don't you, Son?"

Something about the way my father said that had me smiling.

"Of course, I want him healthy," I said with a straight face. "That'll be perfectly acceptable."

"But, Sir," the nurse in charge said. "That room is occupied..."

I turned my head so my eyes could take her in. She was definitely nervous, but I could tell she didn't want the extra hassle of having to deal with this.

"Then un-occupy it," I snapped.

Her mouth slammed shut.

I walked away and didn't stop until I was outside of Naomi's room Naomi where she was still asleep.

My father stopped next to me, and I crossed my arms and stared at her from the doorway.

She looked so tiny in that large hospital bed.

"After calling around on the labels and packaging surrounding him, it looks like he got some antibiotics from the feed store for his 'goat'," my dad said. "Injected himself, and then passed out from a fever."

Dog and cat bites were notorious for that. Although it'd been only fourteen hours since Butterfinger had protected Naomi, it was enough for the bites she'd inflicted on him to become infected. The different types of bacteria in a dog's mouth that just didn't work with the human body.

"He got enough penicillin in him to knock out a horse," Jessie put in his two cents. "What the fuck would possess him to think that he knew that this was the right amount that he needed? The man weighs two hundred pounds, at most. There's no fuckin' way in the world that he should've ever gotten enough for a five-hundred-pound goat. And who the fuck thinks that a goat weighs five hundred pounds? That should've set off their radar right there."

"I've done that before," Fender interjected, breaking into the conversation. "I was having some problems with some…areas. So, I went to the store, told them I had a calf that was sickly. Got fucked up on some fence. Then shot that shit into my junk once I got home. I was out for like six hours as I tried to recover from the pain."

We all looked at him like he was crazy.

"You've got to be fucking kidding me," I finally said. "What the fuck in the world would possess you to do something like that?"

Fender shrugged. "I was sixteen and wasn't really sure that I wanted the hot nurse to know that I did something to my dick and thought it might fall off."

"You're lucky it didn't fall off," my father mumbled. "Jesus Christ, kid."

Fender laughed. "I'm lucky a lot of stuff didn't fall off. Never once did I worry about my dick like that again, though. If anything happens from now on, I'll just whip it out and show it to Dr.

Biker."

I looked over at Tommy Tom to see what he thought about that.

"Why me?" he asked. "He's a paramedic. And so is she."

Tommy Tom pointed to Naomi where she was lying in bed.

"I don't want to see anyone else's dick but the one that belongs to me."

I grinned and walked back into the room, stopping with my feet only inches away from her bed.

"You finally awake?" I asked, trying to keep the shakiness out of my voice that seemed to be permanently seated there every time I saw her face.

"I've been awake. Just resting my eyes, really."

I snorted and dropped my fisted hands to her bedside, then leaned carefully forward and placed a kiss on her split lips.

"You want something to drink?"

The words left my mouth, and my breath danced over her lips, that was how close we still were.

"Dr. Pepper."

I snorted and pulled back, studying her face.

"I'm not sure that your doctor will allow you to have Dr. Pepper yet. I do have some tasty ice chips for you, though."

She huffed out a breath of air, then turned even further and stared at the men in the hall trying to talk quietly.

"Tell them to get in here and sit down. They're making me nervous."

I looked over at the men where they were standing, all of them like silent sentries protecting the occupants within, and grinned. "I think they like you."

She licked her lips, and her eyelids drooped. "I'm glad you're here, Sean."

"Where else would I rather be but with you?"

Her smile was soft and sweet. "I'm glad this particular nightmare is over."

I also thought that the nightmares were over. Little did I know that they were only beginning.

CHAPTER 23

So it turns out when you're an adult, there's literally no one who can tell you that you can't have cake for breakfast.
-Fact of life

Sean

"The dog saved her life," my dad said. "If it wasn't for her, Naomi would be dead right now, and we wouldn't be talking about what I was bringing for dinner."

That was so true that I couldn't stand it.

I'd hated that dog. I'd cursed that dog. I'd wanted to get rid of that dog.

But then she'd saved her life, and I was going to be stuck with her now.

Not that I was complaining. I'd take her growling at me and snapping at my toes as I passed as long as she'd save Naomi's life if there ever came another time that she'd have to do so again.

"Did you get her to go outside without picking her up today?"

My father nodded.

"Yes," he said. "But the moment I tried to get her back inside, she tried to bite off my hand."

I laughed then. It felt freeing, like I was finally able to believe that my life wasn't going to take a turn for the worse.

It was day four of Naomi's hospital stay, and the pretty colors on her face were finally starting to change colors.

If all went as planned, she would be leaving this hospital this afternoon after her kidney function was tested at the one in the afternoon blood checks.

"You should try to be nicer to her," Naomi said as she rolled over on the bed, facing us. "She kicked ass."

My mouth twitched.

"She did kick ass. She just didn't stop at your attacker's ass. Now she's kicking everyone's ass who isn't me, and since I'm here most of the time with you, my brothers are starting to think this dog is as big of an asshole as I think she is."

All of a sudden, she was laughing, her face a mask of healing bruises, but still relaying the joy that she was feeling.

She was mending.

She had a baby growing in her womb, one that we weren't planning but realized quickly that we both really wanted.

And everything seemed fine.

But when the next her smile slipped off her face, and she was looking down at her lap as if something had fallen into it during her conversation, my laughter faded.

"What is it?" I asked, dropping my half-eaten slice of pizza down onto my plate and staring at Naomi with concern lacing my features.

She opened her mouth to speak, but her eyes rolled into the back of her head.

I stood up, not caring that my plate hit the floor with the move, and took two giant steps toward her.

My hand was yanking on the cord on the wall, the one that called every single nurse and doctor in the vicinity into our room, and started leaning the bed backward as Naomi's bruised body continued to convulse.

"Dad, get a pillow against the side rails so she doesn't slam her head against them, but don't drop them."

My father followed my instructions.

On the outside I was calm, cool and collected.

On the inside I was a churning mess of worry and terror, wound tight into a barely functioning shell.

The nurses rushed into the room, and I was slowly pushed out of the way as I watched helplessly while they started working on my woman.

The sheet and blanket that'd been covering her were thrown to the floor at the foot of the bed, and my eyes went to them, uncomprehending at what exactly I was seeing.

Blood. I know that it looked a lot worse than it was, but it was my girl bleeding. There was blood on them, and I had no clue where that blood was coming from.

But the moment I returned my eyes to Naomi, I realized where it was coming from.

Her thighs were slick with blood. Between her legs, on the sheets beneath her, was a puddle of blood forming on the waterproof sheets that hospitals used to help with cleanup. She had to have been bleeding for a while and didn't realize it.

And that's when I realized that our dose of nightmares weren't finished yet.

The baby that we were both so excited about was now gone, too.

They got her convulsions under control, but the bleeding continued sluggishly.

Naomi's head lolled to the side, and I realized with a start that her eyes were open, and she was staring at me with comprehension filling her eyes.

"I love you," she whispered.

My heart ached and my throat started to tighten.

"I love you, too, baby," I whispered back.

Her eyes closed.

I moved forward and grabbed her hand, despite getting a look by the nurse at the head of her bed, telling me without words that I was in the way.

Her eyes opened once again, distant and lost.

"I want you to move to the land," she rasped. "Take the RV and go. Don't stay at your dad's a minute longer. Build our dream home. Live, Sean."

Then her eyes rolled back in her head, and she lost consciousness for the second time in less than five minutes.

This time, I was a lot less hopeful than the last.

***

"We believe that the bleeding has to do with her having a placental abruption. We have to do an exploratory surgery to stop the bleeding." The doctor was shaking his head. "If we don't, she could suffer some long term affects," he hesitated. "Normally, this decision is left up to the individual, but since you're her fiancé, and she's still under a great deal of stress due to her other injuries, I think this is the best course of action."

My throat convulsed.

The procedure would help her...but it was one that scared the absolute crap out of me. Any surgery was a risk. There were no guarantees.

But as I sat there, and looked at my woman with her too pale face, I realized that I was going to have to make this decision whether I wanted to or not.

"Do it," I said.

And as they wheeled her away, I wanted to scream. To cry. To shout to the world about the injustice of it all.

I settled for walking down the hallway, turning quietly into the room that was being guarded by Aaron, and closing the door so softly behind me that it was only a whisper of a sound.

Aaron didn't stop me, either.

No, he felt my pain. He knew what was going through me right now. He realized that I was a loose cannon, and I needed outlet for everything I was feeling, all the pain and the worry.

I walked quietly over to the bed. Stared down at Walton where he lay comfortably in the bed.

He was handcuffed to it, sure, but he didn't look like he was hurting.

No, he was hooked up to pain meds, had a fuckin' pillow under his goddamn head. He was fed and had the goddamn TV on, while Naomi was being taken to the operating room to have her insides repaired after losing our baby

And I just couldn't handle it all anymore.

I snapped my fist out, and punched him straight in the nose.

***

Three days passed, and on the third day, when I was getting anxious and worried that she wouldn't pull through this, the color started to return to her cheeks.

By that afternoon, her eyes were moving behind her lids.

But still she didn't wake.

"Need you to come get her outside. She had a setback, and I'm worried about her."

I turned my head to my father and stared.

"You think I give a good goddamn about that dog right now, Dad?" I asked. "Let her starve."

I felt light pressure on my forearm, and my eyes automatically flew to the bed.

"Be nice to Butterfinger," she ordered.

I opened my mouth to reply, but nothing came out.

Nothing but a sob, that was.

CHAPTER 24

The check engine light should be more specific. For instance, do I just need to check the gas cap, or do I need to stop right now so my engine doesn't explode?
-Naomi's secret thoughts

Naomi

Life wasn't the same after Sean and I lost the child we didn't even know about.

But it wasn't a bad different. Just not the same as it once had been.

Sean was scared.

He was scared to touch me. Scared to leave me. Scared to let me do my job.

He literally would've wrapped me up in bubble wrap if he thought he could get away with it.

I picked up my telephone and dialed my best friend, hoping she'd give me some advice that would help me deal with this crazy, overprotective man of mine.

It'd been four months since I'd lost our baby, and four months since I'd seen the same man that I'd been sitting next to a hospital bed with, discussing what we would name our child when he or she came.

The phone rang, and not five seconds later my best friend in the whole wide world answered with a frustrated, "Hello?"

The sound of a baby crying in the background made my heart pang.

"I need some help," I said without preamble. "Sean still won't touch me."

"What'd he do now?" she asked warily.

"It's what he won't do. I don't know what to do," I told my best friend. "He doesn't even look at me the same. He doesn't touch me unless it's to hug me, and when he hugs me, it's only long enough to act like he's not trying to get away from me."

I plunked backwards onto the bed, and watched my hot, bearded paramedic mow the front lawn.

Something had to give, and it wasn't going to be me.

She hummed, then cursed succulently. "Fuck you, cocksucker."

"Did you just call one of your kids a cocksucker?" I asked worriedly.

"No," she snapped. "It was Downy's fucking dog. She ate my banana bread!"

I snickered softly under my breath, and then couldn't help it, and busted a gut.

"Oh, God," I wiped tears from my eyes. "She didn't mean to."

"Didn't mean to my ass," she grumbled. "That bitch is a bitch, pure and simple. She watched me the entire time she leaned over my plate and ate it. She knew exactly what she was doing."

Downy's dog was a police K-9 officer and really was a good dog...when she wanted to be.

"Hey," she interrupted my laughing. "I heard that there's another litter of puppies from the same sire that Mocha came from."

My eyebrows lifted.

"Did you ask for his number like I asked you?" I asked hopefully.

"Yep," she confirmed. "And I also got the name of a woman who's married to a supreme badass. Guess what!"

I rolled my eyes to the ceiling and frowned when I saw all of the dust on the blades of the ceiling fan. At least I can say that I've never seen the ceiling fan turned off, so how could I know it was dirty?

"What?" I asked, standing up and heading to the wall where the switch for the fan was and flipped it on and off a few times to see if it was just off.

It wasn't.

Sean had purchased a repossessed mobile home from an auction and had moved it to the land that I now called my own—my own with Sean—a few weeks after I was released from the hospital.

It was the biggest piece of shit that I'd ever lived in, and that was even including my own shitty humble abode where I'd stayed for the first few months of my time in Mooresville. But it was mine and Sean's, and I loved it.

We'd broken ground on a small country-style pier and beam home that was expected to be finished mid next year.

I could see the level pad from the window I was standing next to, and every time I saw the progress of it, I got even more excited.

Sean passed my window again, his face dripping with sweat.

He was wearing faded tight blue jeans, a brown leather belt, his black motorcycle boots, and a frown.

Sweat dripped down the tight planes of his abs, and his eyes were covered in a pair of aviator sunglasses that were literally so damn sexy on him that I wanted to run out and jump on him.

My luck, though, he'd just push me off of him and apologize for doing nothing like he always did.

"Are you even listening to me?" Aspen growled.

My lips twitched. "Yes, sorry, keep going."

"The man that does the dogs is actually part of the Dixie Wardens, but they're out of Benton, Louisiana," she said. "His name is Trance. There's a member's wife that trains the dogs once they're a little older. Helps them become protection dogs."

My lips tipped up into a full-out grin as I made my way down the hall to the kitchen.

Grabbing one of the dusting towels out of the drawer next to the fridge, I headed back into the bedroom and stepped up onto the bed.

The ceiling fan had to be cleaned. If it wasn't going to work, I wasn't going to stare at that disgusting sight.

"You know who I think you need to talk to?" Aspen asked suddenly. "PD."

My brows furrowed.

"What?" I asked in confusion. "Why would I talk to him?"

"Because his wife had her arm lopped off with a sword, and she almost lost their child." She informed me of something I already knew. "If anyone knows what Sean is going through, it's him. He almost lost her multiple times, and he's a man. I'm not a man, so I really wouldn't know what Sean is feeling. I've told you all of the things that I would do, and if those aren't working, then I think you need expert advice."

I blinked, then nodded my head in understanding.

Putting the phone onto speaker, I thrust it into my bra and stretched my arms up over my head

"That's true," I said as I started to clean the blades, gagging slightly when dust fell into my hair. "But I think talking to another man will piss Sean off."

"It will piss Sean off."

I squeaked, whipping around, and in the process jolted the ceiling fan, causing every single piece of dust that was left on it to fall to the bed.

My body teetered on the edge of the bed, and he steadied me with two hands on my hips.

It also fell all over me, and I shivered.

"Jesus Christ, Sean," I gasped, placing my dust rag over my heart. "You scared the shit out of me."

"Why do you need to talk to another man when you have me to talk to?"

Sean's words stopped me cold.

"I gotta go, Aspen," I said, dropping the rag to the floor. "Sean just walked in."

Before Aspen could reply, I fished the phone out of my bra, hit end, and then tossed it to the now dirty bed.

Sean crossed his arms over his sweaty chest, and I swallowed thickly.

The man was gorgeous, even when he was pissed.

And he was pissed. His eyes were hard, his mouth was set in a thin line, and he was breathing heavy despite being in the best shape of any man I knew.

"What are you doing up there?" he asked.

There was so much inferred calm in his tone, and I narrowed my eyes.

"I'm cleaning. What does it look like I'm doing?" I snapped.

His jaw ticked as he clenched his teeth.

Anything that looked even remotely dangerous to the man had him getting this feral 'you won't do it' attitude about him that was seriously getting on my nerves.

"You ready to go?" he asked, staring at me like I was crazy.

I nodded. "Almost. Should I be wearing my boots?"

He shook his head, and I growled. "Sean!"

"What?" he snapped.

"I want to ride your bike with you!"

He was already shaking his head.

"Sean, I'm not spun glass. You can't treat me like I'm an infant who's going to fall over and bump her head around every turn. Treat me like an adult! Please!" I cried out, waving my hand with the dust rag in my hand around as I spoke, causing dust particles to flat in the air around us.

He waved the dust away from his face.

"Naomi..."

I shook my head. "No. Just no. You either let me ride on the back of your bike, or I'm going to stay with my mom for a few days."

"You will not be going there alone."

I was done. So fucking done.

"And, in case you forgot, Walton Whitley is in a medical facility with brain damage. He literally can do nothing to me. If I want to drive six hours to my mother's house, I'll damn well drive six hours to my mother's house."

"We'll go to your mother's house this weekend just like we've already planned," he growled. "And this has nothing to do with Whitley."

Yeah, right.

I'd learned over the last four months what, exactly, Sean had done to the man that was my attacker. He'd punched him in the face for what he had done to me.

Since he'd been what they deemed as 'stable' when he was in the hospital, he wasn't wearing as many of the monitors as he had been. So, sometime after Sean had gone in there and punched him in the nose, the man had started to vomit. He'd suffered irreparable brain damage when he choked on his own vomit. Nobody really knew what had happened for sure since he'd been alone.

I doubted that Sean had noticed that he was in any trouble when he'd left.

Not that I would blame Sean for not helping the man, even if he had known.

I wouldn't have.

Needless to say, the man was in a permanent care facility for inmates, and would be for the rest of his life due to his brain damage suffered from lack of oxygen.

That, I knew, because I'd gone for a visit that Sean still had no clue about and had seen for myself that this man would never be a threat to me again.

A man whose reasons for what he did to me I still didn't know, and I probably never would.

CHAPTER 25

Life has never given me lemons. It's given me anger issues, a love for alcohol, high blood pressure, and an extreme dislike of stupid people.
-Sean's secret thoughts

Sean

I was on my motorcycle, Naomi plastered to my back as happy as she could be, trying not to speed. I was hyperaware. I was freaked way the fuck out, and I didn't want to be riding on my bike with her.

Not because I didn't want her to be there, but because I did.

I liked the way she felt with her body plastered to mine. I liked the way her hair flowed all around us, filling my nostrils with the smell of her.

And honestly, the way her hips were sucked up against my ass made me want to flip her around and fuck her.

God, I was going to hell. I was seriously going to hell.

She wasn't ready. Not yet. Hell, I wouldn't be surprised if she never would be.

But when she dropped her hands to my lap, I nearly drove us off the road.

I'd never, ever been so happy to see my father pull up beside me as I was then.

He didn't say anything to Naomi, but she moved her hands away and looked at my dad.

I was sure her face was flaming.

And as we pulled up in front of the clubhouse, two minutes later, I was trying hard not to laugh when I saw the pink tinging Naomi's cheeks.

It made me feel good that she knew what she'd done and that she still wanted to do it.

Maybe not as badly as I wanted to do it, but it was progress nonetheless.

"Boy," Dad said. "You're late."

I was.

I'd had a fight with Naomi for fifteen minutes, then had to shower and change, before we headed over here.

And that made us over forty-five minutes later.

Luckily, we'd done a lot of the preparations last night, meaning today all we had to do was set the food out and get to cooking the briskets for the annual Dixie Wardens party that we hosted.

Each year, all the chapters got together and had a reunion of sorts. Really it was just a reason to get drunk, eat food, and spend time with extended family. This year there we expected a bigger turnout than in previous years as more people had joined the club and some had married and would be bringing with them their extended families.

So, there'd be plenty of new faces whose acquaintance I hadn't yet made, and a lot of them were already here, mingling with the other members who were also here early.

And though I knew they were all friendly, because they wouldn't be invited by the rest of the club if they weren't, it still made me nervous to let my woman go off in the midst of all of these unknowns.

"Bye, baby," Naomi said as she kissed my bearded cheek. "I'll be in the kitchen if you need me."

Then she was gone, and my father was laughing at me.

"How about you go fuck yourself," I growled.

My father's lips thinned as he tried to stop himself from laughing, but I knew he was doing it on the inside despite the fake façade on the outside.

"Fuckin' A."

Then I lost myself in the crowd, heading toward the back porch so I could help the boys get started on cooking the briskets.

***

My heart was in my throat as I looked around the immediate area for my woman.

"She's over there." That was Ghost.

Ghost who hadn't been the same since that night, four months ago, when he discovered his family missing.

I looked over to where Ghost had pointed and felt my lungs start to work again.

"Thanks," I started forward, then stopped. "You okay?"

He nodded his head, tipped his beer up to his lips, and took a deep pull.

"Fuckin' fantastic."

I didn't reply, taking the words for what they were.

A 'go the fuck away.'

The man had found his wife and child not even a few days after that terrible night that we'd found Naomi hurt, and she had moved in next door to the man who Ghost had told to move.

We all knew it wasn't a coincidence, and Ghost was fighting with himself on whether he should intervene.

I figured it was just a matter of time before it all blew up, and Ghost either did something incredibly stupid or something incredibly smart.

Either way, Ghost would get back what he'd lost, and the entire fucking club would be happy.

Though, I noticed, he was staying out of sight tonight, and I had a feeling it had a lot to do with not wanting to be recognized by another chapter that was here tonight.

Speaking of other chapters, I started toward a man who had one green and one blue eye and was busy chatting my woman up animatedly.

His words were light hearted, and I knew the man was happily married, but it still drove me absolutely nuts to see Naomi talking to some man who wasn't me.

"Sean!"

My eyes went to Naomi's face, and I relaxed slightly.

"Thought you were in the kitchen, baby," I said.

Her smile was spectacular.

"I was, but then I saw this man." She gestured toward Trance. "I heard he has a litter of puppies."

My brows rose.

"A litter of puppies that cost about four thousand dollars a pop," I informed her.

"Oh, no," Naomi said excitedly. "Trance here tells me there's a runt of the litter, one he doesn't think will thrive in police work, and he offered him to me for free!"

Bullshit.

My eyes narrowed on Trance.

There was no way in hell that Trance would get rid of one of his dogs, even one of the runts, for free.

"Is that so?" I drawled.

Naomi nodded excitedly. "Yes! And he said I could have him. All I had to do was come pick him up!"

"Do you really think Butterfinger, the shithead, will allow you to have another dog?"

Naomi nodded. "Yes. She plays well with others. Brady made sure of that."

I watched as Naomi's features went soft as she thought about her old friend.

Brady's murderer was confirmed to be Walton Whitley after his DNA was found at the scene. Apparently, the old man had put up quite the fight.

I smiled as I remembered the proud man.

Brady had left everything he had to us. His house. His car. His substantial nest egg. Everything he had to give, he gave to us. We'd expected his money to would go to his son, but we were wrong—it hadn't. Apparently, they hadn't spoken in a very, very long time.

Of everything that Brady had left us, believe it or not, what I was most thankful for was Butterfinger.

Though the bitch was a bitch, pure and simple, I wouldn't trade her for a damn thing in this entire world. She'd saved my woman's life, and she'd brought her back from the brink of despair and had generally been one of the best dogs I'd ever had the privilege of meeting.

"Then we'll get him," I said resolutely. "Trance, we can stop by on the way home from Naomi's mother's next weekend, if that's okay."

Trance nodded once, and I gave him a look that clearly said I would be paying for the dog.

His lips twitched, and he likely would've said more had he not been called by his wife, who was having trouble with her struggling child.

"Can you please, for the love of God, take this kid so I can help the ladies get dinner on the table?"

Trance took the kid, he had to be about four or five now, and waved his wife on.

"Go on, I got him," he said. "Don't forget to save me some of that bread you made. You know how fast it goes."

She gave him a thumb's up and walked away without answering.

"Guess that's my cue, too," she said, getting up on her tippy toes and pressing a kiss to my jaw. "I'll be in the kitchen if you need me."

I grunted.

"That's what you said last time."

She batted her eyes at me, and had she been slower, I would've caught her and told her just what I thought of that attitude of hers.

But she was fast, and showed not one ounce of pain any longer from the injuries she'd suffered, flouncing away as she tossed me a smile over her shoulder.

I was left, standing there, and watching Trance deal with his handful of a child, wishing that I could have that, too.

But it wouldn't be any time soon…if at all.

***

My heart was still in my throat fifteen minutes later as I found my way to the secluded corner of the yard. Hoping for some peace and quiet as I tried to get my heart to let go of the past and move on.

Not many people knew this was here since it was so dark and far away, and that was the exact thing I was looking for right then.

I was startled to see one of the two chairs occupied, but I sat down anyway, tipped my beer to my lips, and drank.

I wasn't really sure how the hell we got to talking, but I found myself telling the stranger, though he was a familiar stranger who I couldn't quite place, all about my fears and worries.

"I can't fucking breathe when she drives away from me," I told this man who I didn't even know. "Every time I watch her walk toward her car, I have a fuckin' panic attack that she's not going to come back."

The man grunted.

"WW was a fucking douche. If he weren't already close to dead, I'd kill him for you."

My brows lifted.

"Who?"

His smile was small, but there.

"WW. The man responsible for hurting your wife."

I was too stunned over the fact that this man knew Walton Whitley to correct him on Naomi being my wife.

"How do you know him?" I asked, stiffening slightly.

The man offered me his hand.

"I'm Dante, the owner of Hail Auto Recovery."

"Dante Hale. The president of the Hale Raisers," I droned. "I know who you are."

"Unofficial president," he corrected. "We're not a true club, just recreational. That's just what we're called."

I shrugged. "Brothers are brothers, man. You don't have to call the club a club, but you are what you are. If it walks like a dog, acts like a dog, looks like a dog, it's a fuckin' dog."

Dante Hale was the man that everyone in the room was talking about tonight. He was a friend of the Benton chapter's president, Silas Mackenzie. And another member's wife, Ruthie had been best friends with Dante's wife. Until his wife had died about six months ago in a car crash, along with their two children.

Dante had, apparently, gone off the deep end. Even now he was obviously not in the best of shape. Hence the reason for him being in the dark part of the clubhouse backyard, sitting with me for over thirty minutes before either one of us had spoken.

"Walton Whitley was one of the longest standing employees that I had, but he was also in an accident about two years ago. Took his wife and kids." His voice broke on the last three words, and I suddenly wanted to be anywhere but here.

Dante, this big bruiser of a man, was utterly broken.

"I can't say that I would do the same if I found someone who looked like my wife," he cleared his throat. "But I can see it now. I can see it, and I feel like utter shit. But I can see it."

"God. They had the same color hair. The same color eyes. *The same fucking smile,*" Dante's voice cracked as he remembered.

I said nothing.

There was nothing to say.

"Take it from me," Dante's voice cracked. "Don't waste a second."

My heart caught as I heard the emotion in the man's voice. Even though I couldn't see him, I knew that he was on the verge of tears.

I took his words to heart, though.

The moment I got my woman alone tonight, I was done wasting time.

I was going to have her back, and I was going to make her mine forever and always.

CHAPTER 26

Skinny girls shouldn't be in charge of the thermostat. You need a middle-aged woman, thirty pounds overweight, with hot flashes named Bertha.
-Rules to live by

Naomi

I looked at Sean warily.

"Are you sure you're okay?"

In answer, he wrapped his arms around me and placed a wet kiss on my mouth.

Then he pushed me onto the bed and walked away from me, disappearing into the closet.

"What…"

He was back before I could ask him more, and in his hand was a black box that looked like a ring box.

"Sean…"

He dropped down to his knee in front of me, and I forgot how to freakin' breathe.

"Sean…"

"Naomi, two years ago, I didn't believe that I'd ever be here," he said softly, looking down at the ring box that he had in his hand. "I'd been waiting to find the woman I was meant to spend my life with for so long, that I was starting to believe I'd never find her. I'd tried to give my heart away a few times, but no one seemed to want it. Now I know, though, that it was because all along it was meant for you. He looked up. "I didn't know that you were out there, but you have the power to bring me to my knees. But now that I do know how my life can be with you, I don't want to spend another minute without you being tied to me in every single way possible."

Tears started to burn my throat.

"Sean..."

"When you nearly died...when our baby was taken from us," his voice broke. "I nearly followed you."

"Sean, no." I lifted my hand to cup his cheek.

"I want to marry you. I want to have a family with you. I want to build our house, fill it with kids, and scream at them the way my dad and mom used to do to me."

A sob caught in my throat.

"And I want you to be there with me, every step of the way."

I nodded, tears flowing freely down my cheeks.

"Do you want my babies?" he asked. "I would understand if not after..."

"Yes." I placed a kiss on his mouth and pulled back, waiting to see what he said next.

"Do you want to marry me?"

I nodded my head.

"Yes."

"Can we get married tomorrow?"

I started to laugh.

"Yes," I said. "I can call my mom and Aspen right now. They'll all come up here."

His eyes closed.

"I love you, Naomi."

"I didn't break, you know," I said to him quietly.

His eyes opened.

"I didn't break after we lost our baby, because of you. It was your strength, your love, that got me through. Yes, it still hurts sometimes, but I have you. There's not a lot of room in here for pain, because you've filled it full with love." I patted my chest, directly over my heart. "You fought off all my demons, and you replaced all my nightmares with hopes and dreams."

He held his arms open wide, and I launched myself into them.

"Do I get to see the ring now?" I asked him, looking down at him from where I'd pushed him to the floor.

He nodded and held up the box.

I snatched it from him, opened it, and my breath caught.

"It's beautiful, Sean."

"It was my mother's."

Tears ran uninhibited down my cheeks.

"I love it."

He took the box out of my hand, slipped the ring from it, and then pushed it onto my finger.

Where it would stay for the rest of our lives if I had anything to say about it.

My eyes caught his, and I saw triumph in them before he hooked his hand around my neck, brought my lips to his, and finally,

finally, kissed me like he meant it.

Butterfinger growled from somewhere across the room, but I didn't bother looking at her. This moment was mine and Sean's, and I wouldn't let her ruin it.

The bitch.

***

Sean

18 hours later

"Test, test...testicles."

I sighed and looked over at Truth.

"Really?" I asked him, yelling across the hall.

He shrugged.

"It's time for the best man speech," he said.

I wanted to smack him. "You're not the best man."

That was lost on him.

"So?"

I rolled my eyes, pulled my wife into my arms and smashed my lips down onto hers.

"I'm going to kill him."

Naomi's answering smile was enough to make my breath catch in my chest.

"Sean."

I looked over to find Dante standing there, his eyes haunted, but a genuine smile on his lips.

"Hey, man," I said, offering him my hand. "You headed out?"

He nodded. "Yeah. Got a business to run, and employees that think it's okay to jack around when I'm not there."

My lips twitched.

"Then I guess I can understand," I said, dropping his hand. "Don't be a stranger."

He nodded once, then left without another word. Not even to the men who had come with him.

"That's so sad."

It was.

Dante looked like a man who was only existing.

I'd nearly lost Naomi, but that man had lost so much more, it was a wonder that he was still standing.

"You'll watch out for him?"

Naomi's words brought my eyes to hers.

"Yeah, we'll watch out for Dante. I know where he lives."

"Hey, it's time to release her for a dance."

I looked up to find Naomi's brother standing there, his face a mask of unease, and released Naomi. "Go dance with your brother, baby. He looks like he needs it."

And as Naomi got up and walked away, heading to the dance floor with her brother who had shown up with a whipped look about him, I looked around the room at all of our family and friends.

New and old.

And realized rather quickly that I was one truly blessed man.

Standing up, I reached for the microphone that was sitting on top of the speaker, and then reached over and shut the radio off.

Everyone in the vicinity turned my way.

***

Naomi

"A year ago, I was not in a good place. I was a shell of the man that I used to be, and I didn't even realize it."

Sean's words made me turn, and my eyes widened as I looked at my brother.

"I think you're wanted back," he teased.

I pressed a kiss to my brother's cheek, then turned to find Sean staring at me over the length of the half-assed dance floor.

"When you wrote this note to me," Sean cleared his throat. "I was so freakin' mad at you. Had been for weeks. But you just kept chipping away at that hard shell around my heart until you finally broke through. But with this note, you broke *me*."

I hadn't realized that he'd carried it around with him ever since. I hadn't even been sure that he even found it.

That made my heart sing.

The note wasn't really great. But I'd written the words in a last-ditch effort to get past the wall he'd erected. I'd left it for him as I was leaving. I'd placed it on his motorcycle seat with a Hershey's Kiss to hold it down.

I don't want you to be mad at me anymore. I was being stupid. I'm a girl, and we do stupid things sometimes. But ever since I've gotten out of the hospital, you've broken my heart a little more each day. It hurts. I miss my friend. Don't be mad at me.

"I hadn't realized I'd been so mean," he said, talking only to me now, as if there were no one else in the room.

I didn't want him to know that he'd broken my heart with his words and actions over and over again those few weeks I'd stayed with his dad. It'd been torturous and wonderful all at once, and it was something I'd meant to hold onto.

But then I'd seen him talking to his ex and I'd written the note out of desperation.

"You're the only woman I want, and if you leave me all alone on this earth, I'll be like your friend. Lonely and lost, with my heart missing, and the only thing making me put one foot in front of the other would be my inability to disappoint my father."

Brady and Sean were a lot alike, and as I walked across the dance floor to him, I knew that I'd love him as hard as he would let me. Forever and always.

***

Ghost

My heart hurt.

EPILOGUE

Sometimes when I'm mad at my husband, I shave my pubes with his razor.
-Text from Naomi to Aspen

Sean

Four years later

"I bought you a cookie."

I looked over at my wife as she came into the room, and grinned widely at her.

"Thanks baby," I said, heading toward her for a kiss. "Just set it down, and I'll get it in a minute." I held up the blanket. "I need to give this to your kid."

She laughed and started emptying her pockets. Saline flushes. A tourniquet. Cotton swabs and four by four gauze pads. "My kid?"

I ignored that and walked toward the hallway and stopped at the base of the stairs.

Butterfinger snarled at me.

I snarled back.

"Fuck you."

"Sean!" Naomi growled in annoyance. "Don't do that."

I grumbled under my breath.

"Seriously, this is beyond ridiculous," I mumbled, being careful to stay out of Butterfinger's reach so she wouldn't actually make contact with my feet like she'd done hundreds of times before. "Stupid fuckin' dog."

"Daddy," my daughter, Molly, cried out. "Nice."

I rolled my eyes and tossed my girl her blanket.

The moment she had it in her possession, Butterfinger got up off the floor, and walked to the stairs to wait for Molly to gather her hugs before heading to bed.

I walked forward and dropped down to my knees, smoothing Molly's wild curls back from her face. "Now, I want you to promise me that you won't come out of your room tonight. Mommy is tired, okay?"

And Naomi was tired. She was six weeks pregnant with our second child, and had just gotten off a twenty-four-hour shift where she didn't catch but four hours of sleep.

Ever since our daughter was born, we no longer went on the same shifts so one of us would always be home with Molly.

It wasn't the easiest thing in the world to do, but it worked for us.

Though, it helped that Naomi had drastically cut down her hours so that she was only working part time. Meaning, I didn't get to have her two days out of the week instead of four like we had been doing.

Molly tightened her hold on me, and then released my neck to head for her mother. "Goodnight, Mother."

My almost-three-year-old had an attitude. She also liked her daddy better than her mommy.

Not that Naomi minded...much. The girl was just so much like me that it was hard for us not to be close. I was sure the next kid wouldn't like me at all since this one tended to always choose me over Naomi.

"Goodnight, daughter," Naomi chuckled as she shot me a death glare over our child's shoulder. "Make sure you go potty. I'd hate to have to clean up pee in the morning."

Molly widened her eyes and shook her head as if to say 'oh, no she didn't.'

"I don't pee on my bed. My bed pees on me," she snarled in the cutest little cherub voice that had the power to bring me to my knees. "And you, are mean."

Molly turned on her heel and flounced away, passing me with bared teeth. "Don't look at me."

I held up my hands in surrender.

"I…"

"Molly Kate!"

I looked toward the door where my father was coming through, his eyes on my girl as she started up the stairs.

Molly changed directions and started to tumble down the steps in her haste to get to 'Papa'. Luckily, Butterfinger was there, blocking her fall before she could even get more than a teeter in.

"Oh, giiiirl," Dad said as he snatched her off her feet. "I missed you." Dad's grin was soft. "Did you read your books?"

"Daddy read," she nodded. "I just waited for him to finish so I could read."

Molly wasn't a reader…*yet*. She was advanced as fuck, and already as smart as a whip. She had the vocabulary of a fifteen-year-old, and an attitude that could rival any teenager's.

She was so much like me that it was scary. The spitting image, as my father liked to point out.

"Let's get in bed, then," he said as he headed for the stairs.

I waved at my dad as he passed me a humorous look over his shoulder, and headed for the kitchen where I could hear my wife banging around.

"I already did those," I told her.

She dropped the pan and sighed. "Sorry. They were in the same spot. I just assumed you didn't hear me."

I snorted. "You assumed that they were dirty, and that I ignored what you had to say."

"Well..." she grinned. "That's you. I say something, and unless it has to do with sex, beer, guns, or your princess, you completely ignore what I have to say."

I walked up to her and dropped a kiss on her mouth, being sure to rub my beard against her chin once I was finished.

"I listen."

"You listen," she agreed. "When you want to."

I shrugged. "I can't help it that you won't speak to me about stuff that I want to listen to."

She punched me in the chest.

"That was so...so...ugh!"

I grinned and gave her a sound kiss straight to the lips.

She returned the kiss, then pushed away from me and headed for the living room.

"She's mad at me and you."

"What for this time?" Naomi yawned, then fell back onto the couch and slumped into it, closing her eyes and snuggling in like she was there for the long haul.

"Don't forget that we're having the boys and their wives over today."

She cracked open one eye.

"I'll get up and get changed when they get here."

I snorted, then reached down and hauled her to her feet.

Once she was on her feet, I scooped her up into my arms and carried her to our room, winking at my dad as I passed him on the way.

I placed her down on the bed, and she sighed, staring up at the ceiling fan that we'd picked out together a little over three years ago.

"I love this place."

I grinned, looking over at the wall plaque that said the same thing that she said every single time she made it to our room and laid down onto our bed.

Emotion stung my throat, and I repositioned myself between her thighs before leaning over her, hands fisted and planted on the bed on either side of her head.

"This place we've built, you've been with me every step of the way," I rumbled. "You were with me the day we broke ground. You were with me the day the first wall was put up. The first nail was put into the drywall. The first stroke of paint was put on the wall." I took a deep breath. "I'm so lucky that I met you."

Her eyes welled with tears.

"Are you going to say the same thing to me every time I say 'I love this place' to you?"

I grinned.

"I feel like it's a game. Like I have to say it now."

She started to snicker.

I dropped a kiss to her mouth, and she groaned.

"I'm so horny," she said boldly. "I've been dying to have you inside of me all day."

I grinned and pushed away from her, walking to the door and slamming it closed before twisting the lock.

"Don't forget the bathroom door, too," she said, sitting up and stripping her clothes from her body as she spoke, all signs of exhaustion wiped away from her face.

Then again, that wasn't very surprising. The woman' libido was greater than even mine when she was pregnant, and I wasn't a spring chicken anymore.

But my body didn't care, happy to oblige her each and every time she raised the flag of need for me to see.

By the time I stripped my pants off, she was already naked and dropping to her knees in front of me.

By the time I had my hand wrapped around her hair, she was already sinking that hot, silky mouth down onto my cock.

"Jesus Christ, Nay," I groaned.

The woman was a fucking nympho. Always wanting me—my finger and my cock—and I wasn't inclined to think it was a bad thing, either.

Not when she practically sucked my soul out of my cock every time she did this.

It only took four strokes of her hot little mouth before I was pulling her off.

"On your knees," I ordered.

The doorbell rang, but I didn't bother stopping. Not when my woman needed me.

Naomi scrambled to her knees and wiggled her ass, inviting me to take her hard and fast.

That was one thing I didn't oblige her with all the time. Though she may want hard and fast, I wanted slow and sensual.

And that's exactly what I gave her.

***

An hour later, I was sitting on the arm of the couch, listening to my club bullshit about missing wedding rings.

"What do you mean you can't find it?" Fender asked in confusion. "You left it right the fuck there. Your woman's going to fucking kill you."

Laughing at the interaction between the men, I clapped Jessie on the shoulder and said, "You'll never win. Just let it be."

He winked at me, clearly baiting Fender with his words, and cocked his beer in Fender's direction. "Fuck off."

I grinned all the way up the stairs, halting when I saw Naomi sneaking the door of Molly's room quietly closed.

"She pee?"

Naomi's laughing eyes came to me.

"She decided to sleep on the floor with a single blanket than risk her precious daddy getting mad at her again," Naomi pushed the door open for me to see.

I started chuckling.

Our daughter was potty trained...mostly. The only time she wasn't was at night when she had something to drink about two hours prior to bedtime.

And since I couldn't fucking resist my girl's pouty lip, I nearly always gave her the drink despite knowing someone would be doing a shit ton of laundry the next morning.

"That's you coming out in her," I said to my wife, pulling her into the curve of my arm.

***

Sean

Ten minutes later, we were standing in the kitchen, and I was again reminded of how much I loved my wife.

"Are you going to eat that cookie?"

I gave Naomi one long look.

"Yes," I said teasingly, knowing what she wanted. "Why?"

She looked at the cookie longingly, then pursed her lips. "Well, it's just that you let it sit there for over an hour, and I think that if you really wanted it, you'd have eaten already."

I grinned.

"Is that right?"

She narrowed her eyes.

"Now is not the time to fuck with me."

"Pregnant girls get hangry," Imogen said as she fell backwards on the couch, a plate of chips and dip balancing precariously on the top of her swollen belly. "You should just let her have the cookie. If you had wanted it, you would've eaten it the moment she walked in the door with them."

I didn't mention the fact that I'd been kept busy since she'd walked into the door with them.

"You can have my cookie," I told her, knowing I wasn't going to win this one.

Naomi's eyes lit.

"Thank God."

I chuckled as she immediately got up, snatched the cookie box, and proceeded to shove the entire thing into her mouth in less than four bites.

I refrained from whimpering.

It really had sounded good.

"Good, baby?"

"Of course it was good, Son." Dad butted in. "Or she wouldn't be making orgasmic sounds in front of your whole club."

"Your father's right," Naomi said around a mouthful of cookie. "It's really good."

I caught Naomi's hand and pulled her into my lap, licking off a stray drop of chocolate that fell into the crease of her mouth.

"Pretty fucking good," I agreed.

She offered me her finger next, and I sucked it into my mouth.

Her eyes dilated, and I threw my head back and laughed.

"Insatiable."

"Only for you," I growled.

"Get a room!" Came from not one, but five of the people in the room.

That was my club. Always Debbie Downers.

"Oh, my God!" Truth came slamming out of the bathroom. "That shitter stool is the best thing since sliced bread!"

"What's a shitter stool?" Verity questioned her husband.

I groaned and covered my eyes, embarrassment tinging my cheeks with a flush of color.

"The 'shitter stool' is more appropriately named the 'squatty potty' and Sean can't poop without it."

I got up and left, grabbing myself a beer.

I couldn't keep the smile off of my face, though.

The woman might get on every single nerve I had, and eat my last goddamned cookie, but I loved the absolute shit out of her.

And she knew it, if the smile she gave me as I returned to the room was anything to go by.

"You're a shithead," I informed her.

She shrugged. "Yeah, I guess I am."

"But I still love you." I informed her seriously. "Enough to share that cookie that I really wanted, and any in the future that you may want as well."

Her eyes softened, and she offered me the last tiny sliver of cookie, and I took it.

Her smile was contagious, and I tried really hard to forget that the cookie was amazing.

I'd do anything for her. Give her my cookie. My heart. My soul.

Anything.

ABOUT THE AUTHOR

Lani Lynn Vale is married to the love of her life that she met in high school. She fell in love with him because he was wearing baseball pants. Ten years later they have three perfectly crazy children and a cat named Demon who likes to wake her up at ungodly times in the night. They live in the greatest state in the world, Texas. She writes contemporary and romantic suspense, and has a love for all things romance. You can find Lani in front of her computer writing away in her fictional characters' world...that is until her husband and kids demand sustenance in the form of food and drink.

Made in the USA
Lexington, KY
23 July 2017